# lowji discovers AMERICA

### CANDACE FLEMING

Atheneum Books for Young Readers
New York   London   Toronto   Sydney

For Allie Nicole, who wanted chapters

Atheneum Books for Young Readers
An imprint of Simon & Schuster Children's Publishing Division
1230 Avenue of the Americas, New York, New York 10020
This book is a work of fiction. Any references to historical events,
real people, or real locales are used fictitiously. Other names, characters, places,
and incidents are products of the author's imagination, and any resemblance
to actual events or locales or persons, living or dead, is entirely coincidental.
Copyright © 2005 by Candace Fleming
All rights reserved, including the right of reproduction
in whole or in part in any form.
Book design by Kristin Smith
The text for this book is set in Charter.
Manufactured in the United States of America

10 9
Library of Congress Cataloging-in-Publication Data
Fleming, Candace.
Lowji discovers America / Candace Fleming.— 1st ed.
p. cm.
"An Anne Schwartz book."
Summary: A nine-year-old East Indian boy tries to adjust
to his new life in suburban America.
ISBN 0-689-86299-7
[1. Moving, Household—Fiction. 2. Landladies—Fiction.
3. East Indian Americans—Fiction.] I. Title.
PZ7.F59936Lo 2005
[Fic]—dc22
2004006899

# ACKNOWLEDGMENTS

Special thanks to Dr. Babu Suthar, Gujarati instructor at the University of Pennsylvania's South Asia Regional Studies Department, for patiently answering my endless questions, and to Marina Budhos for her invaluable comments and suggestions.

# ★
# BYE-BYE, BOMBAY

I am Lowji Sanjana. I am a kid. I used to live in the country of India, in the big city of Bombay, in an apartment building with my *ma* and my *bape* and NO PETS! That was the apartment building's rule: NO PETS!

But not long ago—just weeks after my ninth birthday—I learned we were moving . . . far away . . . across the ocean . . . to . . .

"America!" exclaimed Bape.

"America?" I gasped. I did not believe my ears!

How could I leave my grandmother and my grandfather? How could I leave my aunts and my uncles and my cousins? How could I leave my school and my best friend, Jamshed?

I started to cry.

Bape put his arms around me. "Look for the good in our move, Lowji," he said. "Find the silver lining."

I blew my nose. What silver lining? I could not find any silver lining.

It was my friend Jamshed who found some silver first.

"Lowji," he said. "In America you can finally have a dog! A dog who will sleep on your bed. A dog who will play ball with you."

"Yes," I said, slowly beginning to find some silver too. "And a cat! I can finally have a cat to cuddle with. A cat who will purr when I pet it."

"And," cried Jamshed, clapping his hands in excitement, "a horse!"

I raised my eyebrows. "A horse?"

"Of course," said Jamshed. "In America many people have horses for galloping across open plains and rounding up cows."

"How do you know this?" I asked.

"I saw it at the cinema," answered Jamshed.

"The cinema?" I thought about the American films I

had seen lately. "I do not remember seeing any horses . . . or cattle . . . or plains."

"Well," admitted Jamshed, "it was an old movie. Really old. In black and white."

"Ah." I nodded. I had never thought of owning a horse before.

Later, when I asked Ma and Bape about having a dog and a cat and maybe even a horse in America, they said, *"Najare padvum."* That means "We will see" in Gujarati—the language we sometimes spoke in Bombay when we were not using English. And so I came to America with high hopes of becoming a pet owner.

And oh, how different things are here in America.

Different clothes!

Different foods!

Different faces!

One thing, however, has stayed the same. NO PETS are allowed in my new apartment either.

Already I have learned an American expression for how I feel about this: *Bummer!*

★

# HELLO, HAMLET

I squash my nose against the taxi window to get a better look at my new American town—Hamlet, Illinois. Hamlet, I see, is small and quiet. I am not used to small and quiet. I am used to big and loud. I am used to honking cars and rattling trains and double-decker buses that raise clouds of hot, dry dust. I am used to sidewalks crowded with shoppers and pushcarts and people asleep on the pavement. I am used to billboards and bridges and buildings that stretch to the sky.

But Hamlet has none of these. Instead it has narrow streets and shady trees. It has a town square with a pizza restaurant, a shoe shop, and a statue of a man on a horse.

"Do people in Hamlet have horses?" I ask.

I hope.

I pray.

But Ma shakes her head.

"Bummer," I say, trying out my new American expression. I flop back against the car seat. I think about the dog I will not be sleeping with. I think about the cat I will not be cuddling.

Our taxi turns a corner, and Bape says, "Look, Lowji, there is the school you will be attending."

I look.

We pass an empty brick building with a playground in the back and a sign in the front. The sign reads: HAMLET ELEMENTARY SCHOOL.

"Where are all the kids?" I ask.

"They are on holiday," answers Bape. "For the summer."

"The whole summer?" I gasp. I do not believe my ears! In Bombay I went to a private school. I went all year-round. I went six days a week.

I can almost hear Jamshed: *More silver, Lowji. More silver!*

I agree.

Then the taxi turns another corner and comes to a stop.

*"Maarun miithun madhurun ghar!"* cries Bape. "Home, sweet home!"

We climb out of the car and stand on the sidewalk.

"What do you think?" asks Bape.

I think I am surprised. In Bombay we lived on the forty-seventh floor of a modern apartment building. Here in Hamlet we will be living on the third floor of an apartment house—a house with a wide front porch and a yard full of trees and grass.

"I like it," says Ma.

I look around. I do not see any balls. I do not see any bicycles.

"Do any kids live in this apartment house?" I ask.

Bape shakes his head. "The letter I received said there are only two other tenants—an elderly lady named Mrs. Pendergast, who lives on the first floor. And a newly married couple with the last name of Dove. They live on the second floor."

I sigh. "No pets and no kids."

My parents do not answer.

The first thing I notice when we step through the front door is that our apartment house is very clean. The walls are as white as Bape's cotton shirt. The floors are shiny. There is not a speck of dust on the stairs or a single cobweb in the corners.

"Lemony fresh," I say, using an American expression I have learned from watching television. "Our apartment house smells lemony fresh."

"It should," someone says, "what with all the elbow grease I put into it."

We turn. A woman wearing men's coveralls and a tool belt is standing there.

"Good afternoon," Bape says politely. He brings his palms together in the Indian gesture of greeting. "We are the Sanjana family. I am Farokh. This is my wife, Sooni. And this is our son, Lowji."

Ma and I nod.

The woman grunts. "The new tenants, huh? Your boxes have been arriving for days now. I've been stacking them in your apartment. Place looks like a warehouse—lots of work for sure."

Ma steps forward. She smiles and asks, "And you are . . . ?"

"Crisp," says the woman. "Ada Crisp. I'm the landlady."

"We are happy to meet you," says Ma.

"Uh-huh," says Landlady Crisp. She takes in Ma's bangles and nose ring. She looks up and down at Ma's *salwar kameez*. Then Landlady Crisp tugs up her tool belt. "Well, I got work to do. If you folks need me, you'll find me in my basement apartment—that is, if I'm not scrubbing, sweeping, or fixing something around here." She stamps away.

And the door to the first-floor apartment flies open.

A white-haired lady pokes her head into the hallway.

"What's going on?" she demands. "What's happening?"

"We are moving in," says Bape.

"We are your new neighbors," says Ma.

"Are you Mrs. Pendergast?" I ask.

"Mind your own business," she says. She slams the door shut.

Ma and Bape and I look at one another.

Then Bape shrugs. He leads the way up the very clean staircase to our third-floor apartment.

★

# FIVE-TOED TRAIL

Right away we begin unpacking. Soon our new apartment is a big mess. Boxes are everywhere. Some are open with our things spilling out. Others are still taped shut. A pile of crumpled newspaper is growing in one corner as Bape unwraps what we have shipped from India.

"Aha!" he cries. He pulls a wooden-framed portrait from a box. "The family!" He acts like he has found buried treasure.

And in a way he has. Because Ma and Bape and I are Parsis—believers in a very ancient religion—we are close to our family. *All* our family. Generations and generations of our family. In Bombay their portraits covered the walls of our home.

Now I watch Bape unwrap single portraits, dual portraits, portraits of people at weddings and *navjotes*. Out come my aunts . . . my uncles . . . my grandparents on their wedding day. Grandmother is wearing a silk sari. Grandfather has on a *fehtna*. Next comes a yellowing portrait of long-ago cousins, followed by my granduncle as a child wearing a white suit. Finally, a group of women I do not recognize comes out of the box.

Bape places each of the portraits carefully on the floor.

"It is too bad Roopa is not here," I say. "Roopa could help you hang the family."

Bape flattens the now empty box. "We do not need Roopa," he says. "We can get along by ourselves."

I am not so sure. Roopa was our servant back in Bombay. She helped us bring up the milk bottles in the morning and clean the dishes in the afternoon. She served our meals and answered our telephone and washed our dirty clothes.

I sigh.

Roopa helped make our apartment a home.

By the doorway of my new bedroom I see a stack of boxes marked LOWJI.

"Ma," I say. "I am feeling sick."

Ma lays a cool hand on my forehead. "You are not feverish," she says. "Where does it hurt?"

I point to my stomach. "It is feeling all tight and ticklish," I say. "And I am hot and a little dizzy. Could I have caught some rare American disease?"

Ma's lips twitch. "You do not have a rare American disease," she says. "You are not sick."

"I feel sick," I say.

Ma puts her arm around my shoulders. "It is not easy to move."

"It is easy for you," I say. "You have a good job at Ace Computers."

"No, Lowji," she says. "It is not easy for me. I may have found a wonderful new job, but I miss Bombay. I miss the aunts and uncles and cousins. I miss Grandmother and Grandfather."

"And I," Bape adds, "miss the Restaurant Tanjore. Hamlet, Illinois, does not look like the kind of town that will be needing a gourmet chef."

He pauses. His eyes start to twinkle. And—uh-oh!—

I know what is coming next. A joke. One of Bape's silly jokes. I brace myself.

"Why are chefs hard to like?" he asks.

"I don't know," Ma answers with a grin. "Why are chefs hard to like?"

"Because they beat eggs, whip cream, and mash potatoes!" Bape snorts and slaps his knee.

Ma giggles.

But I groan. I do not feel like joining in their joking. I do not feel full of fun.

Ma puts her hand on my shoulder. "Come and unpack your boxes, Lowji," she says. "It will make you feel more settled."

I do not need to settle. What I need is a pet. A waggy dog or a purring cat. But I do not say this. Instead I push the stack of boxes through the doorway and into my new bedroom. I open the top one and begin to pull things out of it. My old life is everywhere.

It is like I am an archaeologist on a dig. I can look in the box and I can tell much about myself.

I pull out my rock collection.

*This is a boy who likes science.*

I pull out my colored paper and drawing pencils.

*This is a boy who likes art.*

At the bottom of the box is a card my schoolmates gave me before I moved. Master Bannerjee, my school-teacher, pasted a photograph of the class inside it.

*This is a boy who used to have friends.*

I look at the photograph and see myself smiling in the front row. Next to me is Jamshed. He is smiling too.

"Aha!" shouts Bape from the other room. "Underwear!"

Ma sees me holding the photograph. "Wait until school starts in September," she says. "You will make many friends in September."

Her words do not make me feel better. September is at the end of a whole summer. What will I do for a whole summer with no kids and no pets?

I wipe my eyes and look out my window. From here I can see a grassy field and, beyond that, a cluster of trees. Is this the woods? I have never spent time in the woods. Once, we took the train all the way across India to Bengal. Along the way we visited a nature reserve on the Ganges River. There is a jungle there, with tigers and monkeys. But no woods.

I decide to take a closer look.

"I am going outside," I tell my parents.

"That is the spirit, Lowji," says Bape. He waves a rolling pin he has just taken from a box. "Do not wait for the world to come to you. Go to the world."

Ma takes the rolling pin away from him. "Do not go far," she says. "Do not be gone long."

"I won't," I say.

The woods are wild, and if I am very quiet, I can get close to squirrels and rabbits. I also see a *skunkudio,* a skunk, and even though there are no skunks in India, I know not to get close. I know to stay far, far away.

Along a trickle of a creek I find footprints I think belong to a deer, but I do not see one. I also find another set of footprints. Small footprints with five toes.

A kid's footprints!

I follow them up the muddy bank, around a patch of thorny bushes, and over a fallen log. In a thick patch of weeds I lose sight of the footprints. I look around and—yes!—I find them again in an open spot between two tall fir trees. But how strange. The footprints are suddenly replaced by a set of handprints. Do kids in America walk on their hands? I do not think so, but—wait—just as suddenly the handprints are gone and the footprints are back.

I smile and let the footprints lead me under a tall tree with branches that droop to the ground. I let them lead me over a small stone fence. I let them lead me . . .

Nowhere.

The footprints are gone.

I search for them everywhere. I search for a very long time. But all I find is nothing.

I feel frustrated.

And disappointed.

But most of all I feel curious—very, *very* curious.

# NO PETS!

The next morning I wake up in my new bed, in my new room, in Hamlet, Illinois, U.S.A.

From the kitchen I hear the sounds of crumpling newspaper and cupboard doors banging.

"Aha!" shouts Bape. "Mixing bowls!"

I lie back on my pillow and let my eyes wander over my things, trying to get used to seeing them here.

Last night when I returned from the woods, Ma helped me settle my room. We put my clothes in the closet and my red elephant quilt on the bed. We put my rock collection on one shelf and my school photograph on the other. We piled my colored pencils and paper on the top of my desk.

I can see the colored paper and drawing pencils now. They remind me of my aunt Pareen back in Bombay.

Aunt Pareen makes magic with a piece of colored paper. She folds the paper. She fans the paper. She turns the paper into a star or a sailboat or a thousand other things. She claims folding paper is an ancient and very sacred art form. Once, she shared her sacred art with me. She showed me how to make wishes come true.

I climb out of my bed and reach for a pencil and a piece of red paper. Then, sitting cross-legged on the floor, I write: *I wish I had a pet.*

I fold the red paper the way my aunt showed me— lengthways and sideways and back and forth. When I finish, I have a red bird—a red bird with my wish folded in its wing.

I put on shorts and a shirt. I brush my teeth and my hair (but not with the same brush). Then I take my bird outside. I need a place to set it free.

In the backyard of the apartment house is a table. I climb on top of it and wait for a good breeze.

When it blows, I toss my bird high into the air.

*"Ud!"* I whisper. "Fly!"

The bird goes with the wind. Up. Up. Up.

It drops to the ground. Down. Down. Down.

It plops into the grass.

"Stop messing up my yard! And get off my table!"

Landlady Crisp is standing in front of me.

"I am sorry," I say. I hop down. "I was flying my wish."

"Wish?" says Landlady Crisp. "Looks like trash to me."
She picks up my red bird and crumples it in her fist.

My wish is now a wad of paper.

And I am shaking like a leaf in a windstorm. I am
scared, but I am also angry. I do not like my wishes to
be squashed. I force myself to be brave and say,
"Landlady Crisp, I would like to ask you a question."

"I got no time for questions," she says. "I got work
to do."

She turns and heads inside.

But I am determined. I straighten my shoulders and
follow her. I follow her into the hallway, where a bucket
of lemony fresh bubbles is waiting.

"Landlady Crisp," I say.

"Are you still here?" she asks. Her words snap like the firecrackers Bape and I light every Indian independence day. "What do you want?"

I take a deep breath. "A pet," I say. "A dog."

"No pets!" says Landlady Crisp. She scrubs the floor.

"A cat?" I say. "A cat would be nice."

"No pets!" she says. She scrubs harder.

I pause. I do not think I should ask for a horse, so instead I say, "A hamster? A gerbil? A teeny, tiny mouse?"

"No! No! No! For the last time, NO PETS!" She tosses the scrub brush into the bucket. Lemony fresh bubbles splash over my sandals.

"Why?" I ask.

"Animals are work," she says. "And I got enough work as it is."

"But I would take care of my pet," I say. "You would not have to do anything."

"Oh, wouldn't I," she snorts. "Animals scratch the woodwork. They spot the carpets. They dig up flowers and stink up hallways. Who do you think has to fix all that, huh?" She points to her chest with a soapy finger. "Me! That's who!"

My straight shoulders begin to sag. "I guess I will be lonely until school begins," I sigh. "No kids and no pets!"

Landlady Crisp wipes her hands on her coveralls. "Listen, kid," she says in a voice that is not so snappy. "I feel bad for you. I really do. But when Mr. Crisp died, he left me this whole building to take care of by myself. It's a lot of work, more work than I can ever get done. I can't do more than I already am."

Now it is Landlady Crisp's turn to sigh. "What I wouldn't give for an hour to myself, to put up my feet or visit a friend or just do nothing at all. That would be paradise. . . ." Her voice trails off. The hallway grows quiet as a temple. Then she shakes her head. "Enough!" she snaps. "I got work to do. Get out of here, kid. Go on! Scat!"

Another American expression. And even though I have never heard that word before, I understand what it means.

I scat.

# ★
# ONE-STOP SHOPPING

Aha! Spoons!"

Bape is still in the kitchen when I return.

Ma is at her new job at Ace Computers.

I make my way through my new living room. Already our things from Bombay have been mixed in with the flowered sofas and shiny glass tables that came with our apartment. Now our bright Persian rug covers the floor. Our hand-painted screen covers the window. Above the television set hangs Bape's antique brass plates, and on the shelves sit Ma's collection of English porcelain poodles.

"I wish you dogs were real," I say as I rearrange a

group of black and pink ones. Then I step over a pile of crumpled newspaper and sit on one of the tall kitchen stools.

"Good morning, Bape," I say.

Bape nods hello.

"Do you want some help?" I ask. "Would you like me to stay and help you for a while?"

"Well . . . ," Bape says.

I know he does not really want my help. Because Bape is a chef, he is very particular about the way his kitchen is arranged. He will want to do everything by himself.

"Let's talk while I work," he says. "Where did you go this morning?"

I do not feel like telling him about my wish bird. Or Landlady Crisp. Instead I say, "Outside."

"That's nice," says Bape. He leans down to the bottom of a tall box. I can see only his legs.

"Aha!" he cries. He pulls his head out of the box. "Measuring cups!"

I hop off the stool. "I'm going to watch some television." I sigh. "Perhaps a cartoon. Or a game show." I shuffle toward the door.

"Wait," says Bape. He puts out his hand to stop me. "I had not planned on doing this today, not with the kitchen still unorganized, but . . ." He smiles. "Let's go shopping."

"Shopping? For what?" I ask.

"For this and that," says Bape. "New homes need lots of this and that."

He puts the measuring cups into a cupboard, and his wallet into his back pocket.

We start out.

The sun shines up at us from the sidewalk as we make our way across town. It is hot, so hot that even the patches of shade feel like heavy wool blankets.

"How much farther?" I ask.

"No farther," says Bape. He points. "We are here."

"Here" is a very big store with a very crowded parking lot.

We walk closer.

On top of the very big store stand some very tall letters. The letters spell ALL-MART.

As we approach the front door, it slides open like
magic.

*Swoosh!*

In Bombay there are many shopping malls with
many modern conveniences—escalators, elevators,
automatic doors. But many times these modern conveniences do not work. The escalators do not go up.
The elevators do not come down. The automatic doors
refuse to swoosh.

"Can I try it again?" I beg.

Bape nods.

*Swoosh!*

I step out the door.

*Swoosh!*

I step in the door.

*Swoosh!*

*Swoosh!*

"It works every time!" I shout.

When I am finally through the door for good, I see

a lady wearing a green vest and a big smile. Pinned on her vest is a name tag that says, THELMA STORE GREETER.

"Welcome to All-Mart," chirps Thelma Store Greeter. She frees a cart from a long line of them and rolls it toward us.

We push the cart into the store.

I do not believe my eyes!

All-Mart has everything! Under one roof!

I can hear Jamshed as we roll past Personal Care Products: *More silver, Lowji!*

It really, truly is.

In Bombay we did most of our shopping in our neighborhood. We went to the fruit wallah's shop to buy tomatoes and oranges and tissue-wrapped mangoes. We stopped at the bookstall to buy the *Times of India* and *TV Guide.* We popped in at the chai wallah's shop for a glass of mint tea. And we went to the *halwai* shop for cans of Thums Up soda, pistachios, and cellophane-wrapped packages of raspberry-filled cookies.

At every shop and stall Bape haggled for the best

price. "You ask eight rupees for this?" he would say to the vendor. "I will give you four."

"Four rupees?" The vendor always pretended to be insulted. "How will I feed my family if I give you such a bargain? No, I must have seven rupees."

"Five," Bape would say.

"Six," the vendor would reply.

This haggling would go on until both men agreed on a price. Then the vendor would wrap our purchase in newspaper and place it in our shopping bag.

"Shopping is hard work," I said after one especially long haggling session.

"It certainly is," agreed Bape.

In All-Mart there are no stalls.

There are no cans of Thums-Up.

There is no one haggling.

"One-stop shopping," I say, repeating the All-Mart motto. "I like it."

I begin to hum as Bape and I pass Family Shoes, Small Electronics, Sporting Goods, Pets and Supplies. . . .

Pets?

Pets!

"Bape," I cry. "Can we stop? Can we look at the pets?"

"You go ahead," answers Bape. "I will be right here in the next aisle looking at Bed and Bath items." He pushes the cart away.

And I wander into Pets and Supplies.

I pretend every fish, every rodent, every bird, is mine. I *chit-chit* into the hamster cage, smile into the canary cage, stick my finger into the rabbit cage, and—ugh!—step far away from the snake cage. To be honest, snakes make me shudder. Then . . .

"POOP!" somebody screams in an angry voice. "POOP! POOP!"

I turn.

It is a parrot. A parrot sitting in a wire cage. A wire cage with its door wide open.

"Hello," I say.

The parrot hunches his shoulders and glares at me with yellow-rimmed eyes. "POOP!"

I shake my finger at him. "You are being a very rude bird."

The parrot clacks his hooked beak.

"What is your name?" I ask. "Do you have a name?"

The parrot gets quiet. He cocks his head from one side to the other.

"TIPPY!" he suddenly squawks. "TIPPY IS A GOOD BIRD!"

He ruffles his feathers. He spreads his wings. He flaps and—uh-oh!—he lands on my head.

"POOP!"

I hope he does not.

Tippy's toenails dig into my scalp. He yanks my hair. He nips my ears.

And I love it! Love it! Love it! Until . . .

Three boys come talking and laughing down the aisle.

Two of the boys are brothers. I can tell because they look alike. Both have shaved heads and bruised knees. The third boy is not a brother. He is taller and wearing a baseball cap. All three, I think, are close to my age.

The boys see Tippy and me. They stop talking. They stop laughing. They look me up and down.

I give them my biggest smile.

And guess what?

They pretend like I am not there. They stare right past me. They walk right past me too.

Then the boy in the baseball cap calls, "Where's that poopy parrot?"

And guess what else?

Tippy stops nipping my ears and yanking my hair. He abandons my head for Baseball Cap's.

"That's our bird," says Baseball Cap in an extra-loud voice. "That's our friend Tippy."

The boys glance at me out of the corners of their eyes. And mine begin to burn.

"POOP!"

I hurry into the next aisle.

"Ah, Lowji," Bape cries when he sees me. "Just look at all these bargains!"

His shopping cart is overflowing with "this and that." He tosses a toilet lid cover onto his pile.

"Please," I beg. "Can we go now?"

"Soon," says Bape. He sets off with the cart.

I am no longer humming as we roll past Office Supplies, Infant Clothing, Ladies Underwear.

As we go, I look up and down the aisles.

Luckily I do not see those boys.

In Lawn and Garden, Bape begins searching the shelves.

"Pots and soil," he mumbles. "Pots and . . . aha! Soil!" He grabs a bag of dirt and loads it into the cart. "Soil for our kitchen garden."

Back in Bombay, Bape and I always planted a garden. Not a big backyard garden—Bombay is too crowded for big backyard gardens. No, Bape and I grew a little inside garden. We grew green chilies and coriander, curry leaves and tiny onions. We kept the pots on the windowsill.

Later, when the plants were grown, Bape mixed them with other spices and sprinkled them in his coconut rice and his yogurt salads and the flat, round bread we call *rotli*.

I ask, "What kind of plants will we grow here in America?"

"Flavors from home," answers Bape. "I brought many seeds from India."

I grow quiet for a minute, thinking, and then I

31

ask, "Will seeds from India grow in American soil?"

Bape nods. "They will grow and flourish."

I am not so sure. Still, I take a stack of clay pots from the shelf and add them to the cart, then follow Bape to the cash registers.

As we go, I look up and down the aisles.

# IRONMAN

There are long lines of people waiting at the cash registers. Each person is pushing a cart. Each cart is filled with this and that.

Bape plucks a magazine from a rack. "This is going to take a long time."

I shift my weight from foot to foot.

I read some magazine headlines:

MAN PECKED TO DEATH BY PELICANS

ALLIGATOR BOY SAVES PRESIDENT

EAT CHOCOLATE AND LOSE WEIGHT

I look around for Baseball Cap and his friends.

Then I remember seeing a bench just outside the store's sliding door.

"Bape," I say. "I am going to wait outside."

"Do not go anywhere else," he says. He opens the magazine and starts reading about those pelicans.

*Swoosh!*

I am outside.

I weave my way toward the bench—around plastic wading pools, swing sets, and lawn mowers. When I come to the barbecue grills . . .

I do not believe my eyes!

A very fat pig is sitting in the very hot sun. She is tied to the leg of a charcoal grill.

The pig looks up at me with big brown eyes. She pants a little, and pants a little more.

A woman comes up behind us. "That pig'll be pork roast soon," she says.

"Pork roast?" I am confused. "This pig is not tied *on* the grill," I say. "She is tied *to* the grill."

The woman shakes her head. "I'm talking about the heat. The sun. No water." She shrugs. "Pork roast." She pushes past me and into the store.

I reach down and pet the pig between her pointy ears. "Are you pork roast?" I ask.

The pig makes a choking sound. Her pink tongue flops from her mouth, and I know this pig needs to get inside All-Mart, where it is cool and shady.

I untie the rope, then give it a tug. "Come, pig," I say. "Come with me."

"Gruh," snorts the pig. She heaves herself to her hooves, takes a wobbly step forward, and . . .

Oh, no!

The pig faints!

I drop to my knees and pat her snout. "Wake up, pig! Wake up!"

She does not open her eyes.

I wrap my arms around her plump body and lift.

Ugh!

My arms are not strong enough.

I grab the first person that passes by.

"Help," I yell at a gray-haired man. "This pig has fainted."

"Eh?" says the man.

"This pig," I repeat. "I need help with this pig."

The man's eyes narrow. "What is this?" he asks. "Some kind of joke?"

"No," I say. "This is no joke. This is serious business. This pig is roasting. This pig has fainted."

"Who do I look like?" the man growls. "Old MacDonald?" He stamps away.

And I am feeling confused.

Who is Old MacDonald?

Then the pig makes a snuffling sort of sound, and I am back to feeling worried.

What should I do?

What should I *do*?

That is when I see it.

A dolly!

I have seen dollies back in Bombay. I have seen workmen use them to move heavy things like crates and bricks and . . . and . . .

Pigs!

Quick, I push the dolly over to the limp pig and carefully slide the platform under her very round body.

The pig groans as I tip the dolly backward.

*Oomph!*

It is hard work pushing a passed-out pig on a dolly. The wheels do not want to go straight, and the pig keeps slipping off, and my not-so-strong arms need to stop and rest often. But finally, finally—*swoosh!*—I push that pig through the doors and into the cool air of All-Mart.

I unload her next to the bubble gum machine.

"*O bap re bap!*" I say, which is my favorite Gujarati expression. It means "Thank goodness!"

The pig smacks her dry lips. "Gruh," she says.

Nearby is a stack of blue bottled drinks. SPORTSADE, says the label. I grab one.

That is when the store manager appears. I know it is the store manager because he is wearing a name tag just like Thelma Store Greeter's, except his says, MR. WIGG STORE MANAGER. Pinned beneath his name tag is a blue ribbon. WINNER OF THE ALL-MART FRIENDLINESS AWARD, it reads.

But Mr. Wigg Store Manager is not looking very friendly. "Who let a pig in here?" he shouts. "Who let a dirty pig in here?"

I step forward. "That pig is not dirty," I say. "That pig has fainted."

I hear snickering behind me. I look. It is those boys again.

But I do not have time to worry about them, because Mr. Wigg Store Manager is getting less and less friendly. "You can't bring a pig in here! Don't you know that? It's against the law to bring a dirty, germy animal into a public place. People could get hurt. People could get sick!"

His loud voice and waving arms attract much attention. Not only are those boys watching, but people coming into the store are watching too. Even Thelma Store Greeter is watching.

And I am turning hot, hotter than Bape's curry sauce.

I am turning red, redder than my elephant quilt.

I am wishing I could run, run and hide, when . . .

"Whatcha doing with my pig?" booms a deep voice.

A man charges toward us. He is a huge man. An enormous man. *Vah!* A Himalayan Mountain of a man! His bulging arms are as big around as I am, and his bulging legs are even bigger. Balanced on his wide, wide shoulders are two enormous shopping bags. And stretched across his broad, broad chest is a shirt that reads, IRONMAN. He scowls.

Behind me those boys stop snickering.

"Look at the muscles on that guy," says one brother.

"Man, I wouldn't want to tangle with him," says the other brother.

"Let's boogie," says Baseball Cap.

*Swoosh!*

I am wanting to boogie too. Or scat. Instead I watch Ironman come closer and closer.

My stomach tingles. My knees shake. I jump when Ironman shouts, "What's going on here?"

Mr. Wigg Store Manager pushes me forward. "Why don't *you* tell him?"

I look from Ironman's toes way, way up to his head. "Your p-p-pig was almost p-p-pork roast," I stammer.

Ironman growls.

I stumble on. "It was hot. In the sun. Without water. Your pig was panting. Your pig was fainting."

Ironman's mouth drops wide open like the entrance to the caves at Chandrapur. "Blossom fainted?" he whimpers. "But how? I only left her for a few minutes. I didn't realize . . ."

He drops his bags, then drops to his knees.

Out of his bags roll a red rhinestone collar, two boxes of Cinnamon Oat Toasties, a book called *Eighty-two Exercises for Your Eyelids,* and a pair of running shorts.

Ironman cradles Blossom in his lap. He makes cooing sounds.

Blossom smacks her lips again.

"A drink!" Ironman hollers. "My baby needs a drink."

I hand him the SportsAde.

He opens the bottle with a quick twist, holds Blossom's mouth open, and pours some in.

"Hey!" shouts Mr. Wigg Store Manager. "Who's going to pay for that?"

Ironman growls again.

Mr. Wigg Store Manager backs away.

And Blossom blinks.

"Whoooeee!" whoops Ironman. "You're okay now, aren't you, Blossom baby? You're going to be just fine, aren't you?"

"Zoooeee," Blossom squeals weakly.

"Oh, my little oinky-boinky! I love you sooo much!" gushes Ironman.

And he gives Blossom a great big kiss on her great big snout.

# ★
# AN AFTERNOON FOR SIGHING

The walk back to the apartment house feels even longer and hotter than before. Longer because of the five heavy bags we are now carrying. Hotter because of what happened with those boys . . . and that pig.

I tell Bape all about Blossom and Ironman and Mr. Wigg Store Manager.

When I finish, Bape exclaims, "Lowji, you have had an adventure. Your first American adventure!"

I groan.

I hope there will not be a second American adventure.

In our apartment Bape begins unpacking and organizing again.

I watch him humming and working. And suddenly,

more than anything, I want to plant our kitchen garden.

I drag out the bag of soil we bought.

"May I do this?" I ask.

Bape nods and opens a drawer. He takes out a bag of seeds. "See?" he says. "Flavors from home."

I open the bag and pour the seeds into my hand.

Green chilies. Coriander. Curry leaves. Onions.

I line up the clay pots on the kitchen table and scoop dirt into each one. Carefully I press the seeds into the soil. I pat moist soil over them, then add a little water.

When I place the pots on the windowsill, I whisper, "Grow!"

Then I sigh, and sigh again.

I am in a very sighing mood.

I go into my bedroom and flop onto my bed. My first full day in Hamlet, Illinois, U.S.A., has been a long one.

I remember my wish bird.

*Crumpled.*

I remember those All-Mart boys.

*Ignored.*

I remember Mr. Wigg Store Manager.

*Not friendly.*

And I cannot help it. I sigh again. Then I reach beneath my bed and pull out my photograph book.

My photograph book is filled with pictures. Pictures of my aunts and uncles, grandparents and cousins. Pictures of my apartment building on Colaba Causeway and of my school, Saint Ignatius Academy. Pictures of Jamshed by himself . . . and with me.

When I learned I was moving to America, I was afraid I would forget the faces of my friends and family, so I made this book.

Sometimes I talk to the people in the pictures as if they are really here.

Today is one of those times.

I flip to a picture of Jamshed.

"I am a little sad," I say. "America is full of pets— mice, cats, parrots, even pigs. But I will not be owning any of them."

I look at the picture. It was taken when our class went to the Bombay zoo. Jamshed is grinning. He has a piece of cotton candy stuck in his hair.

I go on. "To be honest, I am more than a little sad. I really need a furry friend. Or a feathered friend. I would even be happy with a scaly, slithery friend."

I can almost hear Jamshed laugh as I say that. He knows how snakes make me shudder.

The thought makes me smile—a little—and then I say, "Any kind of friend would be good."

In the picture Jamshed is still smiling.

"Jamshed, I am out of practice for making friends," I say. "I have not had to do it since my first year at school, when I met you. And I did not even have to think about it then. Making friends just happened."

Another sigh slips out.

"Do you think it will happen here in America?"

Jamshed says nothing.

"I do not think so either," I say. "No furry friends. No feathered or scaly friends." I sigh again. "No friends at all."

★

# A MYSTERY AND A MOUSE

I feel better the next morning after a big hug from Ma, a big helping of Bape's eggs scrambled with spices and onions, and—uh-oh!—one of his silly jokes.

"If Hungarians eat goulash and Mexicans eat tacos, what do Chinese eat?"

I shrug.

"Chow mein-ly!" howls Bape. "Get it?" He punches me in the shoulder.

I roll my eyes. But now, instead of sighs, I am full of energy. I am ready to take another walk in the woods. Maybe, I think, I will find the owner of the five-toed footprints.

I take a piece of *rotli* from a plate on the counter and head out.

But on the second-floor landing I see the newly married couple—the Doves. I know it is them because they are gazing at each other with starry eyes . . . and because there is a bird-shaped plaque on their door that reads:

THE LOVEY DOVES
TOM AND MICHELLE

The Lovey Doves are too busy with each other to notice me. They hug good-bye. They kiss good-bye. And—blech!—they hug good-bye again.

I try not to gag as I hurry past them.

Safe in the woods away from all that hugging and kissing, I break the bread into pieces and toss them to the birds. A squirrel jumps down from a tree. He shakes his tail at the birds, scattering them to the sky. This makes me think of my red wish bird that was squashed by Landlady Crisp. Do squashed wishes come true?

I wipe the crumbs off my hands and try to ignore the tight and ticklish feeling that is growing in my stomach again. Instead I look for new footprints. I look beside the creek. I look along the stone fence.

And I find lots of footprints—squirrel footprints, raccoon footprints, skunk footprints.

Bummer!

I do not find any new kid footprints.

I am trudging back toward the apartment house, past the fence and the droopy tree, when I see them—dozens of them—scattered all over the ground.

Little.

Brown.

O-shaped.

They seem familiar.

I pick one up and sniff it.

It smells sweet.

I lick it.

It tastes sweet.

And all of a sudden I know what these are. I have seen them advertised on television. I can even sing the commercial. I sing it now:

> *"What's cinnamon sweet*
> *and so good to eat,*

*the happiest, healthiest breakfast treat?*
*It's Cinnamon Oat Toastieeeeeees!"*

I hold the last note until the birds start flapping and the squirrels start chattering. Then, as my voice fades, I start to wonder.

Are these Oat Toasties meant to be a trail? A trail through the woods like in that story "Hansel and Gretel"? Maybe, I think, someone needs the cereal to find their way home.

But no.

This is not a cereal trail. This is a cereal spill.

Why would someone spill their cereal way out here in the woods?

Then a squirrel scrambles past my feet. He stuffs his cheeks with Oat Toasties.

Now I understand! Someone else is feeding the animals too. Someone who likes cereal.

Could it be the same someone who leaves footprints and handprints?

"This," I say out loud, "is a mystery."

I ponder this mystery all the way home. But the minute I step into the apartment house, all mysterious thoughts vanish because . . .

A mouse is running down the hall!

Landlady Crisp is running after it. She swings a broom.

The door to the first-floor apartment flies open. "What's going on? What's happening?" demands Mrs. Pendergast.

"Mouse!" cries Landlady Crisp.

"Eeek!" cries Mrs. Pendergast. She slams the door.

"Landlady Crisp," I cry. "You have gotten a pet!"

"That's not a pet," she pants. "That's just more work." She aims and swats.

The mouse escapes through a crack in the floorboards.

"If it's not one thing, it's another," huffs Landlady Crisp. She stamps down to her workroom, and I follow.

Downstairs Landlady Crisp searches through cabinets until she finds some mousetraps.

"What are those for?" I ask.

"I'm going to have to catch the filthy pests," she

answers. "Oh, what a lot of work it will be. Baiting. Setting. Waiting. Emptying. Over and over again. It will go on for weeks. After all, where there's one mouse, there's fifty, you know."

"I did not know," I say.

"It's true," she says. "It will take hours every day. You can bet your sweet bippy on it."

Sweet bippy? Even though I have not heard that American expression before, I am pretty sure I know what a bippy is. But is it really sweet?

I try not to giggle as Landlady Crisp moans, "How will I get it all done? How?"

I know she is not asking me. I know grown-ups talk to themselves all the time. They ask themselves questions that they do not expect anyone to answer. But I *do* have an answer. It is a perfect answer.

"A *bilaadi*!" I cry. "A cat! Landlady Crisp, you need a cat. In Bombay people who have cats do not have *undardis*—mice."

Landlady Crisp looks up from her mousetraps. "A cat?" she repeats.

"Yes," I say. "A cat would save you much work."

*Snap!* goes one of the traps.

"OUCH!" hollers Landlady Crisp. She shakes the trap off her thumb.

"Cats do not get caught on fingers, either," I say.

Landlady Crisp turns. Her eyes are like blue ice.

I take a step backward. "It is time for me to scat," I say. I move my sweet bippy up the stairs.

But the next morning before I walk in the woods, I walk down to the basement. I want to see if Landlady Crisp has caught any mice. I open the workroom door and . . .

I do not believe my eyes.

There is a cat sitting on the table. A green-eyed, gray-furred cat. The cat licks a white-tipped paw, then rubs it over a white-tipped ear.

"Mew," says the cat.

"Landlady Crisp," I cry. "You have gotten a pet. Can I have a pet too?"

"This is not a pet," she replies. "This is a super-deluxe mousetrap."

I rub the cat between the ears. She purrs and rubs

me back. "She is very affectionate for a mousetrap," I say. "Does she have a name?"

Landlady Crisp snorts. "Do I name my wrench? Do I name my toilet plunger? No. That cat's a tool just like all the rest. It doesn't need a name."

I watch the cat leap off the table. It weaves in and out and around Landlady Crisp's ankles.

"That cat likes you," I say.

"Humph," says Landlady Crisp. But she bends and runs her hand down the cat's silky back.

"You know what you should name that cat?" I ask. "You should name her Trapper."

Landlady Crisp straightens. "Trapper, Snapper, Blapper," she says. "One name's as good as another. Now, get lost, kid. The cat's got work to do."

"Get lost?" I say.

"Scram! Beat it! Scat!"

"Or boogie." I grin.

"Go," growls Landlady Crisp.

I go.

★

# I MEET THE KING

I am sitting on the front steps of the apartment house the next afternoon. It is one of those hot summer days when everything stands still. I do not know what to do with myself.

If I were in Bombay, I would know what to do with myself.

I would bicycle with Jamshed up Malabar Hill to climb the rocks at Kamala Nehru Park.

Or I would go to the Regal Cinema.

Or I would wander over to the Restaurant Tanjore, where Bape—if he was not too busy—would give me a bowl of *pista kulfi*.

But what to do here in Hamlet?

I think about taking another walk in the woods, or

maybe another look at my plants, when Ironman and Blossom jog down the street.

Ironman is wearing his new jogging shorts from All-Mart and a shirt that does not have any words on it. His muscly arms pump up and down. They match the pumping of his muscly legs.

Blossom is wearing her new rhinestone collar from All-Mart. It flashes in the sunlight as she waddles far behind Ironman. With her big, flat snout she snuffles under bushes and in flower beds. She eats the tops off every dandelion in her path.

I wave.

Ironman jogs over, then jogs in place.

"Whoooee, it's a small world," he huffs. "You're on my workout route."

"Workout route?" I ask.

Ironman jogs and nods. "We run down Tremont Street every morning."

"Zoooeee!" squeals Blossom.

Ironman goes on. "You left so quick the other day that me and Miss Piggy here never got a chance to say thanks."

"I was happy to help," I say.

"All the same," says Ironman, "I can't thank you enough. This little porker means the world to me, you know? If something had happened to her . . ." He winces. Then winks. "Maybe someday we can do something for you. In the meantime, take care, kid."

They jog and waddle away.

Now the minutes really creep. I watch the grass grow. It does not grow fast.

"Today is a slow day," I say out loud.

Just then a girl on a blue bicycle rides past. She is wearing yellow shorts and a green shirt, and she is pedaling so fast her braids fly out behind her in the breeze.

I wish she would look in my direction. I wish she would look at me.

But she does not notice me at all.

She just pedals away.

I lean back and watch the grass grow some more.

The girl rides by again. And this time she is not using her hands. This time her arms are sticking straight out at her sides.

I am impressed. Her trick reminds me of the tightrope walker I saw last year when the Russian circus came to Bombay.

I clap.

But the girl still does not look at me.

She pedals away again.

I stand, walk to the edge of the yard, and wait. I hope the girl will ride past again.

And guess what?

She does!

And guess what else?

She looks at me as she pedals slowly past, this time gripping the handlebars. She looks at me . . . and looks at me . . . and looks at me, even when she has to twist her neck to do it. Before she turns the corner . . . she smiles!

And I grin. I hope she comes back. I will smile at *her* this time. Maybe I will even say hello.

I wait and wait, but she does not come back.

I think about going upstairs and reading a book—maybe *Tales of King Arthur* or *Charlotte's Web.*

Hmmm.

Maybe Landlady Crisp will let me play with her cat. It will, I think, be more interesting than grass.

I go inside.

Downstairs the workroom is cool, and it smells of Landlady Crisp's cleaning supplies—lemony fresh.

"Hello!" I call out.

Landlady Crisp looks up from a lamp she is fixing. "You again?" she says. "Don't you have something else to do besides bother me?"

"I have nothing else to do," I say sadly. "And no one to do it with."

"Humph," Landlady Crisp snorts. But she does not tell me to scat. She does not ask me to get lost or beat it.

I unfold a chair and sit in the room's corner. Trapper creeps out from under the tool bench. She rubs against Landlady Crisp's ankles before springing into my lap. I scratch under her chin.

Landlady Crisp ignores us both. She turns the volume up on her radio.

For a while in the cool, lemony basement there is only me and Trapper, Landlady Crisp and the radio.

Then a song comes on and Landlady Crisp sings along with it. "You ain't nothin' but a hound dog, cryin' all the time. . . ."

"Hound dog?" I ask. "Who is this hound dog?"

Landlady Crisp stops singing. She looks as if she has forgotten I am here. Then she remembers and frowns. "You mean to tell me you've never heard this song before?"

I shake my head.

"But it's Elvis Presley!" she exclaims.

"Who?" I ask.

Landlady Crisp drops her screwdriver and slaps her forehead.

The sound startles Trapper. She leaps off my lap and dashes under the tool bench.

"I can't believe it," cries Landlady Crisp. "You've never heard Elvis Presley? Why, Elvis is the King."

"The king of what?" I ask.

"Of rock and roll!" she howls. Then she turns quiet. She does not speak again until the hound dog song ends. Then in a softer voice she says, "Mr. Crisp and I were crazy for Elvis. We used to buy all his records—

59

danced to them right in our living room. Even after thirty years of marriage we danced."

"That is nice," I say.

"That's all over with," says Landlady Crisp. She gives herself a little shake, and the soft voice falls away. "No time for that sort of nonsense now. Not with all the work around here."

"I am sorry," I say. "I am sorry I have never heard your King Elvis."

"Well, kid, you're going to hear him now." She turns the radio dial up and down, up and down.

"Somebody somewhere is always playing Elvis," she says.

For a few seconds all we hear is *shish-shish-shish*.

Then . . .

"O sole miooooooo!"

"That's sure not the King," says Landlady Crisp. She turns the dial some more.

Then . . .

"I been heartbroke since my country gal's been gone. . . ."

Landlady Crisp winces. "That's not him either." She keeps turning.

"A rash of burglaries have left policemen in Hamlet baffled," says a news announcer.

Landlady Crisp pulls her hand away from the dial. She leans closer to the radio and listens.

"Citizens are warned to lock all doors and—"

"Holy smokes!" shouts Landlady Crisp. "I've got work to do."

"What about the King?" I ask.

"Forget him," she says. "This town's got burglars. And by golly, when a town's got burglars, an apartment house has got to have chains and bolts and burglar alarms. And do you know who's got to install all of that?"

"You?" I guess.

"Me," she groans. "When, oh when, will all this work be done?"

It is another one of those questions grown-ups do not expect to be answered.

But I have the answer. I say, "A *kutto*! A dog! You

should get a dog. In Bombay people who have dogs do not have burglars."

I can tell she is thinking. She rubs her hand over her mouth the way grown-ups do when they are thinking.

"Yes," I say. "A dog would save you much work."

Landlady Crisp's eyes narrow, and I know what is coming next.

"I am going," I say. "Thank you for telling me about the King. Thank you for letting me play with your cat." I bow my head in the polite way Ma has taught me. I run up the basement stairs but stop—surprised—in the hallway.

Where has the slow afternoon gone? Already it is time for dinner. I know this by the long shadows outside and the smell of Bape's chicken masala inside.

I follow the smell to our apartment. Suddenly I am very hungry. It is hard to wait, but Bape keeps me busy. He asks me to set the table. He asks me to wash my hands. Finally Ma comes home and dinner is served.

Mmmm! Mmmm!

Bape has fried the masala—the chicken's special coating—until it is nice and red, and he has covered it

with cashew nuts. The rice is flavored with tumeric—
my favorite spice—until it is a golden color, and Bape
has loaded it with tasty bits of onion.

"Farokh," gushes Ma. "You have outdone yourself."

Bape grins at the compliment. "There is even *gulab
jamun* for dessert," he says.

My mouth waters at the thought.

I grab my fork and gobble three helpings of chicken
masala and two *gulab jamun.*

"Aha!" exclaims Bape. "An appetite!"

Ma and Bape beam as I drain the last drops of milk
from my glass.

I wipe my mouth with my arm. "May I be excused?"
I ask.

"Of course," says Ma.

I point to a serving bowl. "May I take a piece of
chicken?"

"Of course," says Bape.

I grab the meat and race out the door. I take the
steps two at a time.

"Here, *bilaadi, bilaadi, bilaadi,*" I call. I dangle the
chicken between my fingers. "Here, Trapper."

"WOOF!"

Two big paws land like an earthquake on my shoulders. One big tongue slurps first the chicken, then my face.

"Get down, you big galoot," shrieks Landlady Crisp. "Get down, I say!"

The dog gets down.

He is big.

And ugly.

His fur is a patchy mess of brown and black, some of it curly, some of it straight. His legs are long. His tail is short. He has one blue eye and one black.

"God has put you together with leftover parts," I say to the dog.

And the dog smiles. He really does! He pulls back his lips and shows all his white teeth. Then he pants, wags his stubby tail, and drools.

The door to the first-floor apartment flies open. "What's going on? What's happening?"

"Dog," calls Landlady Crisp.

"Ick," shouts Mrs. Pendergast. She slams the door.

"Landlady Crisp," I cry. "You have gotten a pet! Can I get one too?"

"That's not a pet," she says. "That's a burglar alarm. And no, you may not get one too." She reaches down and absentmindedly scratches behind the dog's ears.

"What is his name?" I ask.

Landlady Crisp shrugs. "Is it important? I'll call him Spot or Fido or something."

The perfect name leaps into my mind. "You should call him King," I say, "after your King Elvis."

For one second I think Landlady Crisp is going to smile. But she stops herself before it happens. Instead she shrugs. "Why not?"

"WOOF!" barks King.

# URRRRRRRP!

It is Friday night.

Outside kids are playing tag and catching fireflies. I know this because their happy voices float through our open windows.

Inside I am writing a letter.

Dear Jamshed,

America is not so different from what we thought. I told you I wouldn't see a single cowboy riding across the plain, and I haven't.

I have not even seen a plain.

And the only horse in Hamlet is a statue on the village square.

Still, there are some silver things here. They are:

1. Trapper and King, the cat and dog who live in the apartment building. They are cuddly and waggy. I am not allowed to play with them, though, because they are tools.

2. Ironman. He owns a pig named Blossom, is very nice, and talks to me a lot. But he is a grown-up.

3. Kids. Hamlet is full of kids. I have seen them at the store and riding their bicycles, and I can hear them playing outside right this very minute. Too bad they do not want to play with me.

I wish you were here.

Do you wish I was there?

Write back soon.

Your friend,

Lowji

Outside a kid laughs.
Inside I sigh.
Ma and Bape look at each other.
Then Bape shouts, "Bowling!"

"Bowling?" Ma says. "I have not been bowling in years."

"Bowling?" I say. "I have not been bowling ever."

"Come on," Bape says. "It will be . . . a ball!" He laughs at his own joke.

Ma and I groan as we head out the door.

On the second-floor landing I point to the Doves' door. "Why do they never come out?" I ask. "I have seen them only once."

"Newlyweds like their privacy," says Bape. He wraps his arm around Ma's waist and pulls her close. "They like to be alone."

Ma giggles like my cousin Yasmin, who is fourteen and boy crazy.

Bape waggles his eyebrows and gives her a kiss.

Blech! I really wish everyone would stop doing that. What is it about the second floor that makes everyone so sappy and silly?

"Ahem." I clear my throat.

Ma and Bape move away from each other, just a little.

"Are we going or not?" I ask.

"We are," says Bape. He lets go of Ma and leads us down the stairs.

We walk to the Super Bowl on Seventh Street.

The Super Bowl looks disappointing from the outside—just a long, low brick building.

But inside?

*Silver!* I hear Jamshed shout.

The Super Bowl is bright with spinning lights and blinking arcade games.

It is loud with crashing balls and cheering bowlers.

It smells like pepperoni pizza and yesterday's socks.

I twist my neck, looking this way, looking that way, when—what a coincidence!—I see Ironman sitting behind the counter.

"Hello again," he says when he sees me. "You need a lane?"

I nod. On the walk here Ma explained the game of bowling. I know we will need a lane if we are going to play.

"Take lane ten," says Ironman.

Bape pulls out his wallet, but Ironman waves it away. "It's on the house," he says.

"On the house?" I ask. "Who is on the house?"

"'On the house' means 'free,'" explains Ironman. He winks at me. "It's the least I can do after . . . you know."

I grin. A gift!

And another American expression!

I look around. "Where is Blossom?"

Ironman's big face turns all soft at the mention of his pet. "Pigs aren't allowed in bowling alleys, so I leave her at home. Whoooee, I miss her! I get lonely without her, you know?"

I know.

Then Ironman asks us what size shoes we all wear. We tell him, and Ironman puts three pairs on the counter.

"Aha!" says Bape. "Special bowling shoes!"

The shoes are green and brown. They have numbers on the back and . . .

I wrinkle my nose.

"You mean *stinky* bowling shoes," I say. "Now I know why the Super Bowl smells like old socks."

Bape's eyes start to twinkle. "You know," he says,

"getting them to smell that way was no small feet."

All of us—Ma, Ironman, and I—roll our eyes.

But Bape keeps going. "Yes, they really put their heart into it, body and soles."

I have to admit this is pretty funny, but I hold back my giggle. I do not want to encourage Bape's silly jokes. Instead I change into my stinky bowling shoes. They feel big and a little slippery.

"Am I ready?" I ask Ma and Bape. They are putting on their stinky bowling shoes too. "Can we start playing bowling now?"

"Just 'bowling,'" corrects Ma. "You don't *play* bowling. And you'll need a ball before you begin."

She describes the kind of ball I will need, then points me to the racks.

I begin searching.

Some balls have holes that are too far apart. Some have holes that are too small. Some are too heavy or are ugly colors like black or dark blue.

Finally I find one. My fingers do not get caught. It is not too heavy. It is a nice shiny red.

I carry it to lane ten.

"You are first, Lowji," says Bape. "Throw the ball. Aim for the pins."

I watch the man bowling in lane nine. I watch how he throws his ball. I watch his ball knock all the pins down.

"I do not think I can do that," I say.

"Yes you can," says Bape. "All you need to do is try."

I try.

My ball rolls into what Ma calls a gutter.

I try again.

Another gutter.

Hmmm . . . Maybe those gutters are really made of iron. And maybe my bowling ball has a magnet inside of it.

I sit on the bench.

Hmmm . . . Maybe I'm just bad at bowling.

Ma pats my shoulder. "You'll do better next time," she says.

Bape is next. He picks up his ball, aims, and throws.

His ball does not have a magnet.

It goes right down the center of the lane and hits the pin in the middle.

One bowling pin on each side is left standing.

"A split," says Ma.

"A what?" I ask.

"A split is when the pins are separated with a hole in between them," explains Ma as Bape aims his second ball, throws, misses.

"How do you know so much about this bowling?" I ask.

Ma smiles. "When I was at college in Boston, Massachusetts, my American roommates and I bowled all the time. I learned lots about the game. I became a good player."

"Show him, Sooni," says Bape.

Ma's stinky bowling shoes peek out from beneath the pants of her *salwar kameez* as she aims . . . throws . . .

*Bam!*

All the pins fall down.

"Strike!" says Ma. She takes a little bow.

Bape blows her a kiss. "Your *ma* is still the best," he exclaims.

It is my turn again. Ma joins me on the lane and

shows me how to hold the ball, how to approach, and how to throw.

This time I knock down six pins!

"Silver!" I shout.

Bape and I give each other high fives.

Ma laughs. "Where did you two learn that?"

"From television," says Bape. "Want one?" He slaps Ma's hand.

She slaps him back.

He slaps her other hand.

She slaps him back.

He bumps her hip with his.

She bumps him back.

And I shake my head.

I cannot believe them. They are always telling me to act my age—and then they don't act theirs.

While I wait for my parents to grow up and take their turns at bowling, I look around.

I see Ironman still sitting behind the counter. He is squeezing a hand weight and waiting for customers.

I see a lady in the snack shop. She is serving sodas and slices of pizza.

I see—uh-oh—those boys from All-Mart. They are playing a game with a crane that sits in the middle of a glass box full of prizes. The boys try to get the crane to scoop up a prize, like a stuffed animal or a key chain, but . . .

"Bummer!" shouts Baseball Cap.

The crane comes up empty-clawed.

The boys turn away from the game. They see me. And this time they do not ignore me. This time they head straight for lane ten.

"Lowji, it is your turn," Ma reminds me.

I feel the boys watching as I pick up the ball.

*Please, please roll straight.*

I aim.

*Hit the middle pin! The middle pin!*

I throw.

*A strike! Please! A strike!*

It is a gutter ball.

I am too embarrassed to turn around. Instead, I wait for my ball to come back. As soon as it does, I heave it at the pins again. I know it will not knock any down. I do not even try. To be honest, I just want my turn to end. To be more honest, I just want to disappear.

"It's only a game," says Bape as my ball rolls into the gutter again.

I look down at my stinky bowling shoes and make my way back to the bench.

As soon as I sit, the boys begin making rude noises with their armpits.

I try to ignore them.

Then one of them burps.

"URRRP!"

The others join in.

"URRRP! URRRP!"

They burp. And burp. And burp again.

It is a burping symphony.

I remember how Jamshed could burp the entire English alphabet forward and backward. I remember how he won the school-yard burping competition by burping India's national anthem.

"URRRP!"

Their burps attract me like the gutters attract my bowling ball. I have to look. I turn just as Baseball

Cap pounds his chest to bring up a last one.

It is a big one.

It is a smelly one.

It is—"URRRRRRRP!"—right in my face.

"Excuuuuuuse me," says Baseball Cap, grinning.

I cannot take it anymore.

I gulp air. "No," I say. I take another big gulp. "Excuse *me.*"

And I burp right back at him.

"URRRRRRRRRP!"

It is only one, but it is a good one.

"Lowji!" Ma turns around and shakes her head at me.

But those boys think it is a good one too. I can tell by the way they raise their eyebrows and look at one another.

Baseball Cap nods. "Later, gasbag," he says.

The boys laugh and run off.

Then . . .

*Snap!*

The lights on lane ten go out.

Our first game of bowling is over.

I wish those boys had invited me to go with them.

I wish I didn't feel so alone all of a sudden.

And I really wish I had not drunk so much sweet tea at dinner.

I whisper in Bape's ear.

"Over there," he says, pointing.

On my way to the restroom I peek into the snack shop.

And guess what?

Another coincidence!

The girl on the blue bicycle is on a stool at the snack shop counter. She is swinging her legs and eating a hot dog.

Hmmm.

Should I take a chance and say hello?

I pace back and forth in front of the bathroom sinks trying to decide.

Yes . . . no . . . yes . . . no . . .

Yes!

I square my shoulders and step into the snack shop. But . . .

The girl is gone.

And Ironman is here.

He waves me over.

"How's about a soda?" he asks. "On the house?"

I look around one more time for the girl, then slide up onto the stool beside him. Ironman motions for the waitress. She sets a glass of orange soda in front of me and a glass of milk in front of Ironman.

"Milk?" I say. I do not know any adults who drink milk.

"Sure," says Ironman. "Milk's good for bones. Good for muscles. Good for"—he leans forward and whispers—"something else."

"What?" I ask.

Ironman glances around the snack shop to make sure no one is looking. "Watch," he whispers. He takes a big mouthful of milk and . . .

*Pffffff!*

I do not believe my eyes. A foamy river of milk bubbles out of Ironman's left nostril. It stretches down, down, down, until it dangles off the end of his chin. Then . . .

*Sluuuurp!*

He sucks it back up into his nose and . . .

Swallows!

"Gross," gags the waitress.

"Great!" I cry.

Ironman blushes. "It's nothing, just a little trick."

"That is not a *little* trick," I say. "That is a big trick. An amazing trick. A trick I have to learn! Can you teach me?"

I imagine those boys watching as I blow milk from my nose. I imagine them wide eyed and going, "Wow!" I imagine myself saying, "It is nothing."

Ironman breaks into my daydream. "Sure," he says. "All it takes is practice and control."

Practice and control. That does not sound too hard. I listen carefully as Ironman explains how to swish the milk toward the roof of my mouth.

"That's where your nasal cavities are," he says. "Once they're filled with milk, you simply press your right nostril closed, give a firm but gentle blow, and— ta-da!—milk."

"Barf," says the waitress.

But Ironman ignores her. "Now you try," he says. He pushes the glass of milk toward me.

I do not hesitate. I drink, swish, press, and . . .

Oh, no. I blow too hard.

Milk sprays across the counter.

I sputter and cough.

And the waitress shouts, "That's it, Virgil. Enough!" She snatches the milk glass away.

"Virgil?" My words come out sounding milky. "Who is Virgil?"

"I am," says Ironman.

Ironman—I mean, Virgil—slides off the stool. "Back to work." He pats me on the shoulder. "Keep practicing, buddy." Then, with a wink to the waitress, he heads back to his counter.

And I head back to lane ten.

★

# SOMETHING IN COMMON

Nothing!"

I am looking at my kitchen garden a few days later. I am looking in the pots. I am hoping to see a sprout, but all I see is smooth black soil.

"Bape," I say. "I do not think this garden is going to grow. I do not think plants from India grow in America."

"They will," says Bape. "Give them time."

After lunch I decide to walk in the woods.

But on my way out I notice some strange things. There are cobwebs in the corners. There are smudges on the front door. There is dirt on the stairs.

Cobwebs, smudges, and dirt? Landlady Crisp is sick, I think.

But no. When I step out onto the porch, I see her coming down the sidewalk with King. King is on one end of the leash. He pulls from side to side. He runs around and around. His pink tongue hangs out of his mouth and his ears flap. I can tell he is happy.

Landlady Crisp is on the other end of the leash. She is pulled from side to side. She is twisted around and around. Her pink tongue is hanging out too as she tries to hang on to the leash. I cannot see if her ears are flapping, but I can tell that she is *not* happy.

King drags her into the front yard, and she unleashes him.

He plows toward me.

One second I am standing on my feet.

*Oomph!*

The next I am not.

One second I am dry faced.

*Sluurp!*

The next I am drowning in dog kisses.

I giggle.

King *yip-yips*.

And a flash of blue whizzes down the sidewalk.

Could it be?

I wrestle King off my chest and struggle to my feet, but the blue flash is gone.

And so is King. He bounds off to sniff at the trees, the flowers, and Trapper, who is napping on the porch railing.

I sigh and wipe the slobber off my face. Then I look over at Landlady Crisp. She is bent over. Her hands are on her knees and she is breathing as if she has just run the Bengal marathon.

"Good afternoon, Landlady Crisp!" I say.

Landlady Crisp takes one hand off her knee. She flaps it at me—a go-away wave.

"I've got no time for you today," she says between huffs and puffs. "I have to clean out Trapper's litter box, run to the store for kibble and tuna, give King a flea bath, and cut the grass. Of course, before I can cut the grass, I've got to fix the lawn mower. But before I can do any of it . . ." Landlady Crisp flops onto the bottom stair of the porch. "Before I can do any of it, I've got to catch my breath."

She blows in and out a few times, and her shoulders heave.

"Are you all right?" I ask.

"Walking that dog is not easy," she answers. "Walking that dog is hard work."

"If you lived in Bombay, you would not have to walk your dog," I say. "People there do not put their dogs or cats on leashes. There are many animals in Bombay, and they all run free—even cows."

Landlady Crisp raises an eyebrow. "Cows? I don't believe it."

"Believe it," I reply. "Many people in Bombay are of the Hindu religion. Cows are special to them. Cows are—"

Before I can finish, a rabbit dashes out from under the porch.

King dashes after it.

"Woof-woof! Woof-woof!" His bark gets farther and farther away.

"Landlady Crisp!" I cry. "Shouldn't we go after him?"

But Landlady Crisp flaps her hand again—a forget-about-it wave. "You think that dog's gonna get lost? Ha!"

she snorts. "This is the third time he's run off. Mark my words, Lowji, that dog will be home in time for dinner."

"Are you sure?" I ask.

"Sure I'm sure," says Landlady Crisp. "That dog will be fine." She takes another deep breath and changes the subject. "So tell me, are you Hindu?"

"Me?" I glance once more in the direction King has gone, then shake my head. "Lots of my friends are Hindu, but I am not. I am a Parsi—a Zoroastrian."

"Zoro-what?" says Landlady Crisp.

"Zoroastrian," I repeat.

I can tell by the expression on her face that she does not know what a Zoroastrian—called a Parsi in India—is. So I tell her. I tell her how Parsis follow the teachings of the prophet Zarathushtra, who lived three thousand years ago. I tell her how we believe in one God, and how we follow the creed *Humata, hukhta, huvarashta,* which means "Good thoughts, good words, good deeds."

As I am talking, Trapper rises from her sunny spot on the porch railing. She yawns, arches her back, then leaps into Landlady Crisp's lap.

Landlady Crisp pets Trapper under the chin and between the ears.

Trapper purrs.

"Are you feeling rested now?" I ask her. "Should I continue?"

"Go ahead," she says. "Heck, you're better than public television."

Public television?

I do not ask. Instead I sit beside her on the stair. I say, "Two years ago, when I turned seven, I celebrated my *navjote*."

"What's that?" Landlady Crisp rubs her face against Trapper's.

"It is when boys and girls are initiated into the Zoroastrian religion," I say. "It is when we finally get to wear sacred items. I am wearing them now."

Landlady Crisp stops rubbing Trapper and looks me up and down. "I don't see anything sacred."

"That is because you do not recognize them." I pull up my Bart Simpson T-shirt to show her the plain white cotton one underneath. "This is my *sudrah*. I wear it as a reminder to do good deeds." I point to the lamb's-wool belt tied around my waist. "And this is my *kusti*. Wearing it reminds me to speak good words and think good thoughts."

Landlady Crisp looks. She pauses. She finally says, "I wear a reminder too. See?" She pulls a chain out from under her coveralls. On the end of the chain is a gold cross. It glitters in the sunlight.

Now it is my turn to look. And pause. Finally I say, "Landlady Crisp, do you know what this means?"

She shakes her head.

"We have something in common."

"We do?" she asks. "What's that?"

I cannot keep the excitement out of my voice as I exclaim, "We both wear sacred items!"

Landlady Crisp blinks, as if surprised. She looks from her cross to my *sudrah* and back to her cross. "You're right," she finally agrees. "Isn't that the darnedest?"

"It is," I say. Then, trying out my new American expression, I add, "It is the darnedest."

# ON THE FRITZ

Landlady Crisp does not sit and think about sacred things for very long. Soon she tucks her necklace away. She rubs her hand over her mouth.

"What are you thinking?" I ask.

"I'm thinking I got work to do." After one last pat she sets Trapper on the ground, then pulls herself to her feet and walks around to the back of the apartment house.

I follow her.

Trapper follows me.

The lawn mower sits in the middle of the overgrown grass. Landlady Crisp pulls a screwdriver from her tool belt.

"What is wrong with it?" I ask.

"Blast if I know," she grumbles.

She bangs on the motor, then tries to start it. The mower sputters and smokes.

"Of all the . . . ," she growls. "This grass is longer than a cat's tail, and I've got a mower on the fritz."

"Who is Fritz?" I ask.

"*The* fritz," repeats Landlady Crisp. "It means 'not working.'"

"Ah," I say. "Another American expression."

Landlady Crisp stamps her foot. "It's going to take me hours to get this grass cut, and you know what?"

"What?"

"By day after tomorrow it'll need cutting again." Landlady Crisp groans. "Let me tell you. Grass isn't anything but work, work, work."

It is not a question. Still, the answer pops into my head, then pops out of my mouth.

"A *bakrun*!" I shout. "A goat! You should get a goat. In Bombay people who have goats do not have grass."

Landlady Crisp is listening.

"Yes," I say. "A goat would save you much work,

and"—I try out my new expression—"they do not go on the fritz."

Landlady Crisp is thinking, when . . .

"WOOF!"

King comes running toward us. His tongue is hanging out. His tail is wagging. He skids to a stop in front of me.

And here is something strange: There is a key chain clipped to his collar—a key chain like the ones in the crane game, a key chain with a little red bowling ball hanging on it.

I unclip the key chain for a closer look.

*Is this key chain a gift?* I wonder. *A gift for me?*

I think it is.

But from whom?

Maybe Ironman—I mean, Virgil—did this.

"Where did you get this?" I ask King.

He answers by jumping up and licking my mouth.

And here is something else strange: King's kisses do not taste bad!

King's kisses taste *good.*

They taste sweet.

They taste like . . .

Cinnamon Oat Toasties!

I look from King to the woods, then back to King.

"Hmmm," I mutter. "Footprints, handprints, cereal, and key chains."

"What's that you're talking about?" asks Landlady Crisp. She pulls a dog biscuit from her coverall pocket and tosses it to King.

He catches and crunches.

"I am talking about clues," I reply. "Clues to a very mysterious mystery."

I clip the key chain to my *kusti*.

# ★
# FRICK AND FRACK

Even though I have not been in Hamlet, Illinois, for very long, I already have a daily routine.

This is my routine:

I wake up early and eat breakfast. Then I set my plants in the sun and drip a little water into each pot. "Grow!" I whisper.

After that I walk in the woods. I search for more footprints, handprints, cereal, key chains. *Who are you?* I wonder.

I know it is not Ironman. I asked him, and he said he did not know anything about a key chain clipped to a dog collar.

Hmmmm. The mystery deepens.

When I return from the woods, I always sit on the

front stairs and wait for Ironman and Blossom to jog by.

"Hey!" Ironman said only yesterday when he passed. "How's the milk trick coming? Have you been practicing?"

"No," I replied, "Ma will not let me practice in the apartment. She said it was disgusting. And Bape said, 'Everyone *nose* it's *snot* funny to be so gross.' So I have not practiced at all."

"Tough break," said Ironman.

"Uhh," Blossom grunted in agreement.

Then Ironman winked. Blossom ate some dandelions. And they were off—Ironman jogging and Blossom waddling.

Lunchtime is next. Every day I have peanut butter and jelly, like an American kid. Every day I spread the peanut butter and jelly on *rotli* like an Indian kid.

"Ah," says Bape. "The best of both worlds."

I cannot answer because peanut butter, I have discovered, is very sticky.

Then comes . . . the afternoon. Afternoons in Hamlet are like the road to Calcutta—very, very long. Sometimes in the afternoon I watch television.

Sometimes I talk to Jamshed's picture.

Sometimes I sit on the front porch and hope like crazy the girl on the blue bicycle will ride past again.

And every day I try to visit with Trapper and King. Sometimes I bring them little treats. Sometimes I bring them little toys. They are always happy to see me.

"Brr-woof!" barked King when I visited earlier this week. He put his paws on my shoulders.

"Mmm!" purred Trapper. She circled my ankles.

"Go home, Lowji," snapped Landlady Crisp. She waved me away.

"Please," I begged. "I just want to play."

But Landlady Crisp shook her head. "If I've told you once, I've told you a dozen times. These animals aren't pets, and they aren't playmates. They're workers with jobs to do."

As she talked, I could not help but notice the rubber ball rolling across the workroom floor. I could not help but notice the toy mouse dangling from the workroom doorknob.

Hmmm. Could Landlady Crisp be playing with the animals herself?

I doubt it. No, Landlady Crisp is too busy. She has lots of jobs to do. She paints the hallway leading to our apartment. She shampoos the carpeting in the Doves' living room. She fixes the dishwasher in Mrs. Pendergast's kitchen. She is busy every second, scrubbing, dusting, sweeping.

What she is *not* busy doing is mowing. The lawn mower is still on the fritz. The grass is still growing.

Then one morning, as I am gobbling up my second *appam,* my daily routine is changed. There is a knock at our door.

Ma puts down her teacup. "Who would be visiting us so early in the morning?"

Bape puts down his spatula. "Who would visit in the middle of breakfast?"

I put down my fork. "I will find out." I walk to the door and open it.

I do not believe my eyes!

It is Landlady Crisp!

I think she is not believing her eyes either because they grow wide as she looks through the open door at the many portraits, the bright fabrics, and the brass ornaments that decorate our apartment. She sniffs, taking in the fragrant smell of incense.

"Exotic," she says.

Then Ma is at my side. "Landlady Crisp," she says. "What is broken? Have our toilets stopped up? Does the air conditioner not work?" Ma does not wait for an answer. "Farokh!" she calls to Bape. "Landlady Crisp is here to fix the toilets and the air conditioner."

Now Bape is at the door too.

"Nothing is broken here," he says. "The air conditioner is fine, and I flushed the toilet only minutes ago. It, too, works well."

"Holy smokes," snaps Landlady Crisp. "I'm not here to fix anything. I just came to get Lowji."

Now I do not believe my ears.

"You did?" I blurt out. "Why?"

Ma nudges me. "Manners," she whispers.

I try to be polite. "Thank you for coming to get me," I say. But I am feeling very curious. I am too curious to be polite. I hop from foot to foot. I am so curious, I think I will explode.

"Come and join us for breakfast," Ma says.

"Come and try an *appam*," Bape says.

*Oh, no!*

If Bape makes an *appam* for Landlady Crisp, I will be curious for a very long time. Bape will cook and whistle while Ma and Landlady Crisp sip tea. Then Bape will serve his *appams*, and because he is a chef and cannot help himself, he will keep serving *appams*. Landlady Crisp will eat a second and maybe a third.

And I will go *ka-boom* from curiosity.

Luckily Landlady Crisp saves me. "Thanks just the same," she says, "but I got too much work to do. I just wanted Lowji to come and see something if he's got a minute."

I look from Ma to Bape. "Do I have a minute?" I ask.

"Have you finished eating?" Bape asks.

I do not give my second *appam* a second thought. "Yes," I say.

"Then, go," he says. He turns to Landlady Crisp. "Come back soon. I shall be pleased to cook for you."

And Landlady Crisp does the incredible. She smiles . . . sort of. Her thin lips twitch up at the ends, then—quick—they curl back down.

If I had blinked, I would have missed it.

"What are you grinning about?" snaps Landlady Crisp as we head down the stairs.

The real Landlady Crisp is back.

We step into the hallway. It is still dusty, and cobwebs still hang in the corners. When we go down the stairs, I see they are still dirty. And when we pass the laundry room, I see trash cans needing to be emptied and a floor needing to be swept.

I sniff.

Where is that lemony fresh smell?

Outside, the lawn mower is still sitting in the middle of the grass. The grass is still uncut. In some places, though, it is shorter. It looks chewed. It makes me think. . . .

"Landlady Crisp!" I cry. "Did you get a *bakrun*—a goat? Is.that what you wanted to show me?"

"No," she says. "I did not get *a* goat. I got . . . *two*!"

She points to two white goats tied to a tree. Their chin whiskers waggle as they strip bark from its trunk. When I move close, one goat nibbles at the bowling ball key chain hanging from my *kusti*. The other goat tries to strip the sandals from my feet.

"These goats are very hungry," I say. I push them away. "These goats will soon have your grass eaten."

"That and anything else in their path," says Landlady Crisp. She eyes one of the goats, who has turned his attention from my toes to her tool belt.

Just then King races over.

"WOOF! WOOF!"

He sniffs and wags. Sniffs and wags.

"MAAAA!" the goats protest. They bump King with their knobby horns.

"YIP!" cries King. He tucks his tail and runs toward the woods.

"Here, King," I call. "Come back, boy!"

"Let him go," says Landlady Crisp. "You know he'll come home soon."

We turn back to the goats. Their names are Frick and Frack. Frick is the boy. The girl is Frack.

"I do not understand these names," I say. "What do these names mean?"

Landlady Crisp explains that Frick and Frack are

famous characters from a comic strip published in American newspapers in the 1940s.

"But why did you name them after a comic strip?" I ask.

"I didn't," says Landlady Crisp. "The farmer I bought them from did. They already had names when I got them."

"Perhaps," I say, "we can give them new names. Perhaps they do not know the names they have now."

We try out my idea.

Landlady Crisp unties their ropes.

I step back.

But just as I am about to call their names the hairs on my neck start to prickle. My skin starts to creep. Someone is watching me. But who?

I look toward the table where I flew my wish bird.

No one is there.

I look toward the hedge that separates this yard from the next.

No one is there.

I look toward the woods.

Someone *is* there. Someone wearing yellow shorts. Someone peeking through the trees.

Then Landlady Crisp hollers, "Hey! Are you going to call them or what?"

"Oh . . . yes . . . of course," I stammer. I look to the goats. I look back to the woods.

Someone is gone.

And Landlady Crisp is shouting, "I'm ready and waiting!"

I look once more toward the woods, then back to the goats. "Here, Frick!" I call. "Come to me, Frick."

Both goats look up from their munching. Their beards go up and down. Their yellow eyes stare. Then the bigger one—Frick—steps toward me.

"They know their names, all right," says Landlady Crisp.

I scratch between Frick's horns. "Poor goats," I mumble.

"Humph," snorts Landlady Crisp. "These goats have it made. All they have to do is eat and rest, eat and rest. Now, *me,* I've got an entire building to scrub, sweep, and vacuum. I got a dog that needs walking, a cat box that needs scooping, and—"

"I could walk King," I offer. "I could—"

"Eeeeeeee!"

A scream cuts through my words.

"Eew! Eew! Eeeeew!"

"That's Mrs. Pendergast!" cries Landlady Crisp. She races for the building.

I race after her, my mind going faster than my legs.

What is going on? What is happening?

Is it robbery?

Is it murder?

# EEEEW!

It is an *undardi*—a mouse.

To be honest, it is a tiny mouse.

To be more honest, a tiny, dead mouse.

Trapper has left a tiny, dead mouse on Mrs. Pendergast's welcome mat. Mrs. Pendergast found it when she opened her door. Now Trapper is crouched on the mat next to the dead mouse. Her ears are forward. Her tail is flicking. She is watching through the open door as Mrs. Pendergast runs around her apartment.

"Ugh! Mouse! Horrible!" howls Mrs. Pendergast.

She rushes around the living room and through the kitchen with her hands in the air.

"Mouse! Ugh! Mouse!"

Back in the living room again, she leaps onto her doily-covered sofa. "Eeew! Eeew!" She hops up and down with each word.

"Edna," says Landlady Crisp. "Get down before you break a hip."

"Mice!" squeals Mrs. Pendergast. Her finger shakes when she points to her welcome mat.

"Mice are nothing," I say. "You should live in Bombay. In Bombay there are rats. Big rats. Rats in Bombay are this big." I hold my hands far apart.

Mrs. Pendergast has stopped screaming and hopping. She is looking at me wide eyed.

"In Bombay," I say, "many people are Hindu. They do not believe in harming any animals, not even the big rats. So the rats have been given their very own city."

Mrs. Pendergast begins to sweat. She takes a lacy handkerchief from her pocket and pats her forehead and her upper lip.

Landlady Crisp puts a hand on my arm. "Lowji," she says.

"It is true," I say. "The rats' city is in the center of Bombay. Really it is just a big mound of dirt, but the rats have dug tunnels through it. They have built rooms. Thousands of rooms for thousands of rats. And thousands of people visit. It is fun to throw a scrap of food into Rat City. The rats swarm out of their holes. They growl and gnash their sharp teeth and tear—"

"Eeeeeeeew!"

"Now, Edna, calm down," soothes Landlady Crisp. "The boy is just telling a story."

"Yes," I say. "And I am trying to tell you that one little dead mouse is nothing. Thousands of rats—"

"Ugggggh!"

"Is nothing," I say. "In Bombay people visit the rats and nobody screams. Nobody climbs on the furniture."

"Enough, Lowji." Landlady Crisp's words are snapping again. "You are scaring Mrs. Pendergast."

"I did not mean to scare her," I say. "I mean to unscare her."

From on top of the sofa Mrs. Pendergast points

again at the dead mouse. "Get it out of here," she whimpers. "Take it away."

"All right, Edna," says Landlady Crisp. She picks up the mouse by its tail.

Trapper springs at it. She hits it with her paws. The dead mouse swings back and forth, back and forth.

Mrs. Pendergast screams again.

I wish she would stop doing that.

Landlady Crisp wraps the mouse body in newspaper and drops it into a trash can. "There. All gone," she says. She holds her hand out to Mrs. Pendergast. "You can come down now, Edna."

But Mrs. Pendergast digs her heels into the sofa cushions. "How do I know they're all gone? How do I know there aren't mice behind my stove or in my curio cabinet or"—she shudders—"under my bed?"

"This building does not have mice," I say. "This building has a cat, and buildings that have cats do not have mice."

Mrs. Pendergast ignores me. "I just won't feel safe

until you look," she says to Landlady Crisp. "I insist you look everywhere."

Landlady Crisp rests her head in her hands for a moment.

"I will help," I offer.

But Landlady Crisp is not listening. "I knew it," she says more to herself than to me. "Things would have been easier if I had just put out the mousetraps."

She heaves a big sigh, then takes a flashlight from her tool belt and shines it behind Mrs. Pendergast's stove. She finds two pennies, a pot holder, and . . .

"What is that?" I ask.

Landlady Crisp is holding something brown and wrinkled.

"I knew it!" Mrs. Pendergast shouts from her sofa. "Mummified mouse!"

"Mummified pork chop," replies Landlady Crisp. She drops it into the trash can too.

"Oh," says Mrs. Pendergast. She blushes.

Now Landlady Crisp bends and shines her flashlight under the refrigerator. She finds a shriveled carrot, a piece of dried cheese, and . . .

"What stinks?" cries Mrs. Pendergast.

I wrinkle my nose. "Whatever it is must be very rotten," I say. "Whatever it is has been under that refrigerator a very long time."

Landlady Crisp sniffs and her eyes start to water. "That's not rotten food. And it's not coming from under the refrigerator," she cries. "That's skunk!"

# ★
# THE KING STINKS

King is scratching at the front door and whining. His paws are full of mud. His fur is full of burrs. He smells worse than the Ganges River on a hot summer day.

Landlady Crisp pinches her nose and peers at him through the screen door. "This dog has been playing in the woods," she says.

I pull the collar of my shirt over my nose. "This dog has been playing with a *skunkudio,*" I say. "A skunk."

King lifts his tail from between his legs and gives it a hopeful little wag.

"Humph," snorts Landlady Crisp. "Cleaning up this dog is going to be lots of work. It's going to take lots of time."

"Do not forget about Mrs. Pendergast," I say. "She is still hopping on her sofa."

"Holy smokes," mutters Landlady Crisp. "Installing locks and burglar alarms would have been easier than this." She puts her hands on her hips, but only for a second. The stink is too powerful. She quickly pinches shut her nostrils again and says, "Well, first things first."

"What are you going to do?" I ask through my shirt.

"I'm going to use a method from the old days," she says. "But first I need some supplies. While I'm gone, stay here and guard this door. Whatever you do, don't let that dog in the building."

With my free hand, the one not holding my shirt, I grab the doorknob. I hold the door shut. "He will not get past me," I promise.

On the other side of the door King starts howling. He scratches harder.

"Down, King," I say.

King whimpers.

When Landlady Crisp returns, she is wearing plastic gloves on her hands and a plastic rain bonnet on her head. She is carrying a plastic bucket filled with bubbles and has a big can of tomato juice tucked under one arm. "Tomato juice," she explains, "helps get rid of skunk stink."

Outside King has stopped scratching at the door. Now he is poking it with his nose. He *sniff-sniff-sniff*s along the door's bottom.

"Brrr-woof!" He is getting impatient.

Landlady Crisp opens the can and pours the tomato juice into the bubble-filled bucket. The bubbles turn pink.

"Is King going to drink that?" I ask.

Landlady Crisp bumps open the door with her hip and sets the bucket down. "Nope," she says. "He's going to take a bath in it."

At the word *bath* King yelps. He tries to slink away.

But Landlady Crisp is ready. She grabs his collar.

King tugs and pulls, splashing pink bubbles all over the grass . . . all over Landlady Crisp . . . all over me.

"Quick, Lowji," cries Landlady Crisp. "Turn on the hose."

Still covering my nose, I race to where the hose lies coiled like a snake behind a shrub. The rusty handle squeaks when I turn it. A blast of water shoots from the nozzle.

"Lowji!" Landlady Crisp cries again.

"Brrrf! Brrrf! Brrrf!" complains King.

"I am coming!" I shout.

I rush toward them, water gushing in front of me, the hose uncoiling behind me.

King is struggling hard now. And so is Landlady Crisp.

"Squirt him!" hollers Landlady Crisp. "Squirt him!"

I point the hose.

Cold water arches up . . . up . . . and over . . .

"Oops!" I cry.

Soaked to the skin, Landlady Crisp stumbles and falls on her coveralled bottom. Still clinging to King's collar, she pulls the dog on top of her. They wrestle.

I aim the hose again. This time the water hits King in the face. It washes the fight right out of him. All he can do now is tremble. His wet fur makes him look smaller.

Landlady Crisp pushes him off her chest and stands. "Good boy," she soothes. "My King is a good doggy."

She hugs him close until he stops trembling. Gently she rubs the tomato-bubble mixture all over him.

Soon he is covered nose to tail in pink bubbles.

Landlady Crisp says, "Rinse him off, Lowji."

Again I turn the hose on the dog. His eyes look sad as he takes the rinsing.

When all the bubbles are gone, Landlady Crisp soaps him again.

And I rinse him again.

It is past lunchtime when we finish washing King. We sniff his fur.

"I can't say he smells better," says Landlady Crisp. "But he does smell different."

I am thinking King now smells like tomato juice, lemony fresh bubbles, and the Ganges River on a hot summer day. But I do not say this. "Yes," I say, "he does smell different."

Landlady Crisp gives King a kiss on the nose and a dog biscuit from her pocket. Then she lets go of his collar. He dashes away to shake and roll and shake some more.

Landlady Crisp turns off the water. She recoils the

hose. She picks up the now empty bucket and the tossed-aside tomato juice can. "Well," she says. "That chore's done. Now I can get on with—"

"What's going on?" Mrs. Pendergast shouts out her window. "What about my mice?"

Before Landlady Crisp can answer, we hear another shouting voice. A very angry shouting voice. "Whose goats are these? Who owns these monsters of mass destruction?"

"Goats?" gasps Landlady Crisp. "Goats?" She slaps her forehead. "Holy smokes! I forgot to tie up the goats!"

# ★
# HOLY SMOKES!

Landlady Crisp's next-door neighbor is red faced. Veins stand out on his neck, and spit flies as he shouts, "Ada Crisp, are these your goats?"

She starts to speak, but her words are drowned in his anger.

"Do you have any idea what your blasted goats are doing? Do you? They're . . ." He stops. Sniffs. Wrinkles his nose. "What's that smell?"

"The Ganges River," I say.

He gives me a perplexed look, then turns back to Landlady Crisp. "Come with me," he shouts. "Come and see for yourself."

Landlady Crisp tugs the plastic rain bonnet off her

head. Work boots squishing, coveralls dripping, she follows him through the break in the hedge.

I follow Landlady Crisp.

King follows me.

Trapper, who has finally left Mrs. Pendergast's welcome mat, follows King . . . but not too close.

We walk into the biggest mess I have ever seen.

There are shrubs without leaves.

There are stems without flowers.

There are stalks bent and trampled and half chewed.

Chunks of grass have been pulled up. And a clothesline full of laundry has been pulled down.

In the middle of it all stand Frick and Frack. Frick is calmly chewing a pair of striped trousers. Frack is eating a ruffly blouse.

"Maaaa!" say Frick and Frack.

"WOOF!" says King

"Meeeew!" says Trapper.

The next-door neighbor says a word I cannot repeat.

Then Ironman and Blossom burst through the hedge.

"I heard yelling," says Ironman. "I smelled skunk. I

thought . . ." His words trail off at the sight of the destruction. He shakes his head. "Whooeee!"

"Zoooeee!" Blossom squeals.

And King's hair stands straight up. He growls and growls and *woof-woof-woof-woof*s. He shoots across the yard like a furry bullet.

Blossom squeals again and . . .

She runs! Fast! Her plump legs are pumping. Her potbelly is bouncing. She is twisting and weaving and keeping away from King.

"Our jogging has really paid off!" whoops Ironman. He pumps his arm in the air. "Run, Blossom, run!

And Blossom does.

She and King topple the last standing rosebush. They trample the last of the flowers. They drag the laundry through the dirt and tangle it around trees and shrubs.

"Ooops," says Ironman. He chases after Blossom.

"Blast!" hollers Landlady Crisp. We chase after King.

The next-door neighbor says another word I cannot repeat. He chases after us.

Now everyone is either running, yelling, squealing, or barking. Some are doing several of these things.

Trapper hides under the hedge. "Mewww!" she cries.

The goats look up from their shirt and pants. "Maaaa!" they bleat.

As I run, the bright red bowling ball key chain bounces on my *kusti*.

How can Frick resist?

He licks his mouth. He lowers his horns.

*Ooomph!*

One minute I am running, and the next I am flat on my back.

*Crrrunch!*

One minute I am the proud owner of a bowling ball key chain, and the next I am not.

I leap to my feet. "That key chain was a gift!" I cry. "That key chain was a clue!"

Frick does not care. He just chews, chews, chews.

"Look out!" shouts Ironman.

I look.

Blossom is barreling toward me like a runaway bus in the Himalaya Mountains.

"Catch her!" shouts Ironman.

"Grab her!" shouts Landlady Crisp.

"Stop that pig!" shouts the next-door neighbor.

I try. As Frick swallows the last of my key chain, I crouch . . . leap . . .

Yes! I land on Blossom's broad back.

But does Blossom stop?

Oh, no! She is still weaving and twisting and keeping away from King, but she is also bucking and kicking and trying to knock me off.

"Help!" I cry. I cling to the pig as we streak across the patio, tear between two oak trees, and plow into the vegetable garden.

"Not the lounge chairs," shouts the next-door neighbor.

"Watch the hammock," shouts Ironman.

"Holy smokes! No!" shouts Landlady Crisp.

Holy smokes . . . *yes!*

Next to a row of cucumbers Blossom suddenly sinks to her knees.

I jump off her back just as she rolls and rolls.

"My lettuce!" hollers the next-door neighbor. "My green beans!"

"Yip-yip!" King joins in the rolling fun.

"Maa! Maa!" Frick and Frack trot over to feast happily on mashed tomatoes.

"Meow!" Trapper creeps out from under the bush. She flicks her tail and licks her front paw.

"What's going on? What's happening?" Mrs. Pendergast steps through the break in the hedge.

"Goats," roars the next-door neighbor. "I'm infested with goats!"

"And just look at the mess they've made," declares Mrs. Pendergast.

We look.

Frick and Frack are still eating.

Trapper is still licking.

But Blossom and King have stopped rolling. Now they are resting.

King sighs and lays his head on Blossom's jowly neck.

Blossom grunts and nuzzles King with her snout.

"Isn't that cute?" gushes an unfamiliar voice.

We turn, and the Lovey Doves—Tom and Michelle—step through the break in the hedge.

Michelle's eyes grow misty. "They're hugging," she coos.

"And kissing," adds Tom.

"Blech!" I say, gagging.

Landlady Crisp moans. "I knew it. I should have just fixed the lawn mower."

"Fix!" shouts the next-door neighbor. "Fix? You better fix this . . . or else!"

I turn to Ironman. "What is this 'or else'?" I ask.

"Trouble," Ironman answers. His eyes are round as *rotli.* "'Or else' means trouble."

Instead of "or else," Landlady Crisp agrees to fix it all. She shoos everyone—the Lovey Doves, Mrs. Pendergast, Ironman, Blossom, Trapper, King, Frick and Frack, and me—out of the neighbor's yard. She ties the goats to the tree. She puts the cat and dog in her basement apartment. She walks Mrs. Pendergast home and checks behind the elderly lady's washing machine for mice.

Finally she turns to me. "Go home, Lowji. I've got lots of work to do."

"I can help," I say. "I can pick up the dirty laundry. I can push hunks of grass back into the ground."

Landlady Crisp shakes her head.

"I can help around the apartment house too," I go on. "I can empty the trash cans or sweep the stairs."

Landlady Crisp shakes her head again.

"I can help with the animals," I beg. "I can—"

"Stop, Lowji." Landlady Crisp holds up her hand. "Just stop and be quiet."

I get quiet.

Minutes slide by. Finally Landlady Crisp says, "If you really want to help me, stay out of my way." Her voice sounds sad and tired.

"But—," I begin.

"Go home, Lowji." She walks away.

# ★
# MY LAST, BEST IDEA

For the next two days I stay out of the way. I watch TV. I water my plants. I talk to Jamshed's picture.

Meanwhile, Landlady Crisp works without stopping. She washes and dries the laundry. She buys a new pair of striped trousers and a new ruffly blouse. She replaces rosebushes. She repairs the grass. And she replants the flowers and the vegetable garden.

The next-door neighbor stops spitting.

Landlady Crisp groans, "Oh, my aching back."

The third and fourth day, while I still stay out of the way, Landlady Crisp builds a fence. It keeps Frick and Frack out of the neighbor's yard and away from laundry. It keeps King out of the woods and away from skunks.

All the while Landlady Crisp sets mousetraps under Mrs. Pendergast's bed and behind her stove. Even though she knows she will not find any mice, she checks the traps every few hours. This keeps Mrs. Pendergast happy. It keeps her from hopping on the sofa.

"Bone tired," moans Landlady Crisp.

On the fifth day Landlady Crisp finally starts cleaning the mess in the apartment house. I see her bringing out a broom and a scrub brush, a mop and a big bucket of lemony fresh bubbles.

She stands and looks at her cleaning supplies for a moment. Then, instead of sweeping and scrubbing, she crumbles onto the bottom stair.

I cannot stay out of the way any longer.

"Landlady Crisp," I say. "Is everything all right?"

"No, everything is not all right." She takes her hands away from her face and I see she has tears in her eyes. "I can't do it, Lowji. I don't have enough time. I don't have enough energy. There's only one thing left to do."

"What is this one thing?" I ask.

Before she can answer, Frick and Frack start bleating in the yard. They need water.

King appears with his leash dangling from his drooly mouth. He needs a walk.

Trapper crawls from beneath the stairs to meow and meow. She needs a can of tuna fish.

Landlady Crisp blows her nose on her dust rag. "See what I mean? I just can't do it anymore." She leaves the cleaning behind to water the goats, walk the dog, and feed the hungry cat.

The next morning I hear the sound of hammering coming from the front yard.

*What can Landlady Crisp be working on now?* I wonder.

I go outside.

She is pounding a sign into the grass. The sign says: FOR SALE.

"Landlady Crisp!" I cry. "You cannot be selling this apartment house!"

"I don't want to," she says, "but it's either sell the building or get rid of the pets, and . . . well . . ." The lines in her face soften. "I can't do that. Those darn animals have become like . . . like . . . family."

I understand.

"Problem is," she goes on, "I'm so busy taking care of Frick and Frack and King and Trapper that I don't have enough time to get everything else done. The laundry room is full of dust, the stairwells are full of cobwebs, windows are dirty, doors are smudged, and nothing smells lemony fresh." She sighs. "I just can't do it anymore."

No, it is not a question. No, she is not asking for my help. But all of a sudden I have a solution.

"Landlady Crisp!" I exclaim. "Do you know what you need? A pet sitter. In Bombay people who have pet sitters get all their work done."

Landlady Crisp stands very quietly, holding her hammer. I know she is listening.

"Yes," I say. "People who have pet sitters save much time and energy. They do not have to sell their apartment houses."

A smile starts to grow on her tired face, a smile

that she does not fight. "And where," she says slowly, "would I find a pet sitter?"

"I think," I say, "that you might find one right here in your very own apartment house."

Landlady Crisp's smile is now full grown. Her lips curve up, and they stay curved up as she says, "I think you are right."

# ★
# NEW BEGINNINGS

Dear Jamshed,

Everything has changed, even my daily routine. Here is my new daily routine:

1. I still wake up early and eat my breakfast. I still water my plants and whisper, "Grow."

2. I still walk in the woods. I still search for clues and wonder, Who are you? The mystery is still unsolved.

3. I still wait for Ironman and Blossom after my walk in the woods. Ironman is still jogging. Blossom is still eating dandelions.

4. I still eat peanut butter and jelly on rotli for lunch, and there is still . . . THE AFTERNOON.

But guess what?

Afternoons are no longer like the road to Calcutta. Now they are too short. They go by too fast.

Know why?

Because I am very, very busy. I am busy taking care of Trapper and King and Frick and Frack. I have to go take care of them now, but I promise to write more soon.

Your friend,

Lowji

P.S. Guess what? Kids in America are pretty good burpers, but none are as good as you. If you lived in Hamlet, Illinois, U.S.A., you would be the champion burper. You can bet your sweet bippy on it!

I fold the letter, put it in an envelope, and leave it on the kitchen table for Bape to mail. Then, humming, I hop down the stairs to take care of the animals.

First I put water in Frick and Frack's trough.

"Be good goats," I say. I pat their heads.

"Maa!" says Frick.

"Baa!" says Frack.

Next I scoop out Trapper's litter box and fill her bowl with tuna fish.

"Have you caught any mice today?" I ask.

"Meeew!" says Trapper.

I can tell by the way she is gobbling that she has not.

Finally, I take King for a walk.

"Don't go in the woods," warns Landlady Crisp.

"Oh, no," I say. "No more woods for King."

Instead we walk past the town square, with its pizza restaurant, shoe shop, and statue.

We walk past the Ace Computers building, where Ma is working.

We walk past Hamlet Elementary School.

Farther on we come to a baseball field, and guess who is here? Those boys from All-Mart and the bowling alley are throwing and catching and hitting a ball around the field.

While King sniffs a nearby fire hydrant, I watch. I wonder what it feels like to wear one of those gloves for catching balls. I wonder about the right way to hold a bat. I wonder how to play the game of baseball.

On the field one of the brothers sees me. He gets

Baseball Cap's attention, who points me out to the other brother.

For a few long moments all three stare at me.

I stare back at them.

Then guess what?

Baseball Cap burps and . . . waves.

Yes, waves!

I grin. A wave is something! A wave is a beginning!

But before I can wave back, the girl on the blue bicycle whizzes past.

"Brrr-woof!" yips King.

King pulls and pants and runs like crazy after that girl and—*oomph*—I am being pulled. I am panting and running like crazy after the girl too.

But we do not pull, pant, or run like crazy fast enough. By the time we chase across the playground, the girl is gone . . . again.

King whines like his heart is broken. He sits, stares in the direction that the girl has gone, and whimpers, whimpers, whimpers.

I stroke his head. "Poor King," I say. "Why are you

so sad? You do not know that girl, so why are you acting as if you do? Why are you acting like . . ."

King whines again.

And suddenly—suddenly!—I am understanding
things.

I am figuring things out.

I am putting clues together, and . . .

Mystery solved!

# ★
# THE PLACE WHERE WISHES COME TRUE

The next day I race through my pet-sitting chores. I walk King. I feed Trapper. I give Frick and Frack fresh water. Then I hurry out the door and into . . . Landlady Crisp.

"I'm off to visit a friend," she says, "and I'm taking my Elvis Presley records." She opens her bag so I can see.

I hop from foot to foot. "That will be fun," I say. I look in the direction of the woods.

"Want to tag along?" she asks. "Listen to the King?"

I shake my head. "I have already made plans."

"Plans?" she says. "With a friend?"

"I am hoping," I say.

Landlady Crisp raises her eyebrows.

And I shrug. How can I explain that I am off on a

search—a search for a friend? But this is exactly what I am going to do. I am going to look for a friend. And I know just where to find one.

It is very quiet in the woods. Sun shines through the leaves, and the wind is still. I keep my ears open. I keep my eyes open. I am hoping for new footprints and fresh cereal trails.

I look along the trickle of a creek and around the patch of thorny bushes and beside the fallen log. I look next to the stone fence and under the droopy tree. And then I come to the open spot between the two tall firs.

Aha! I see new footprints. I see new handprints. I hear a voice right behind me.

"It's about time you figured it out."

I turn . . . I grin . . . I knew it.

It is the girl on the blue bicycle. She grins back at me.

"Did you like the key chain I sent?" she asks.

"I liked it very much," I say, "until the goats ate it."

We grin at each other some more.

Finally I ask, "Why didn't you give it to me yourself? Were you feeling too shy?"

"No," she says. "I just like to be mysterious."

I nod. Then, remembering my manners, I give her a polite bow. "I am Lowji."

"I'm Tamika," she says.

"I have just moved here from India," I tell her. "Do you know where India is?"

"Sure," says Tamika. "It's in Asia. Elephants and tigers live there, right?"

"That is right," I say. I can tell that Tamika is not only mysterious, but very smart, too.

"Hey," says Tamika. "Can you do a cartwheel?"

I shake my head.

"Watch this," she says. She puts her hands down on the ground and flips sideways. Her feet go up in the air, over, around, and down. Tamika does three cartwheels in a row.

*Vah!* I understand even more! Footprints . . . handprints . . . footprints.

"Now you," she says.

I try to copy her. My hands go down on the ground, I flip sideways, and . . . I fall flat on my sweet bippy.

I wait for Tamika to make fun of me.

But she doesn't. "That's all right," she says. "You'll do better next time."

I can tell that Tamika is very kind.

"I cannot do cartwheels," I say. "But I live in a building with two goats. There is a dog and a cat, too."

"We rent our house," says Tamika. "The landlord says no pets are allowed. That's the rule."

"We used to have that rule too," I say. "But things have changed in my building. Would you like to come and see the animals?"

"Okay," says Tamika. "But I can't stay long. I have a piano lesson today."

We walk out of the woods and across the grassy field to my house.

In the backyard I introduce her to Frick and Frack. Right away Frick chews the bottoms of her shorts. Frack unties one of her hair ribbons.

"No! Naughty goats!" I say, giving them a push. I worry that Tamika will get angry at me for having such bad-mannered goats. I worry that she will not want to play.

But Tamika just laughs and scratches under their bearded chins.

King goes crazy when he sees Tamika. He whines and wags his stubby tail so fast he makes a breeze. When Tamika bends down to give him a hug, he covers her face with his tongue, then *sniff-sniff*s at her pocket.

"Okay! Okay!" laughs Tamika. "But only one." She pulls out a Cinnamon Oat Toastie and tosses it to King.

He catches and crunches.

"You and King are good friends," I say.

Tamika nods and smiles.

Then Trapper comes and rubs herself around and around Tamika's ankles. The cat arches her back and closes her eyes when Tamika strokes her fur.

"You're so lucky," says Tamika. "I wish I could have pets."

I explain that the pets are not really mine. They belong to Landlady Crisp. "But you are always welcome to pet-sit with me," I say.

"Cool," says Tamika.

"You are?" I say. "I will get you a coat."

"No," says Tamika. "'Cool' is another way of saying you like something."

"An American expression," I say, and Tamika nods.

In the apartment I show her my bedroom. I show her my computer and my rock collection and my picture of Jamshed—the one taken at the zoo.

"He looks nice," says Tamika.

Then Bape calls us into the kitchen.

Uh-oh!

"What do you call a cat who eats a lemon?" he asks Tamika.

"A sour puss," she answers.

Bape claps his hands in delight. "Aha!" he exclaims. "A sense of humor!"

Tamika and I giggle as Bape pours us each a glass of cold sweet tea flavored with nutmeg and ginger.

Tamika takes a tiny, tasting sip. "Good," she declares.

"It is my favorite," I say.

We drink our tea and eat the sugar cookies Bape brings us.

Tamika finishes first. "You have crumbs stuck to your mouth," she says.

"You do too," I say.

We giggle again and lick our lips clean.

And suddenly, suddenly I feel good. Really good. I feel like a missing part of me is back again . . . like I am a jigsaw puzzle that once had a big piece missing from its middle but is now whole. Solid. All put together.

Then Tamika looks at the clock. "I have to go," she says.

My jigsaw-puzzle joy breaks into five hundred pieces.

I follow her to the door.

"Thanks for having me over," she says.

"Thank you for coming," I say. But what I really mean is, *This is the best day I've had since moving to America.*

"I had fun," says Tamika.

"I did too," I say. But what I really mean is, *I like you.*

"Bye," says Tamika.

"Good-bye," I say. But what I really mean is, *Come back soon. Please!*

Tamika smiles. She waves. Then just like that . . . she is gone.

Alone, I wander the apartment.

In the kitchen I see the two empty tea glasses still sitting on the table.

*Did Tamika like me?* I wonder.

From the living room window I see the animals still roaming around the yard.

*Will she want to play with me again?*

In my bedroom I see my photograph book still open to Jamshed's picture.

*Will she be my friend?*

I wish . . . I wish? . . . I wish!

Snatching a piece of paper and a pencil off my desk, I write: *I wish Tamika was my friend.* Then I fold the paper lengthways and sideways and back and forth.

Soon a bluebird is sitting in my hand—a bluebird with a very important wish folded in its wing.

I run into the backyard. King chases me. Frick and

Frack look up from the lilac bush they are eating. Trapper flicks her tail.

I jump onto the table and hold up my bird.

*Please, please let this wish fly,* I pray as I wait for the perfect wind.

When it finally comes, I toss my bird into the air.

*"Ud,"* I beg. "Fly."

And it does.

My wish goes with the wind. Up. Up. Up.

"Yes!" I shout.

My wish drops toward the ground. Down. Down. Down.

"No," I moan.

Then—

*O bap re bap!*

A sudden breeze snatches the bird. Shwoosh-whoosh! It carries the bird high. Higher. Higher still.

I shade my eyes and watch my wish go. I imagine it flying with the wind. I see it soaring above the clouds, past the sun, to the place where wishes come true.

"What are you doing?"

Tamika is standing in front of me.

"I was making a wish," I say. I hop off the table and look to see if Tamika is laughing at me.

But she is not laughing. Instead, she is giving me a serious look. "Your wish," she asks, "did it come true?"

I pause a moment before I say, "I think so."

"I'm glad," she says. Then she adds, "My piano lesson was cancelled. Do you still want to play?"

And suddenly I feel good again. Really good. So good I cannot keep it inside. "Tamika," I shout, "you are cool!"

# ★
# GROWING AND FLOURISHING

The *dhansak* is a spicy memory, and the pans are soaking in the sink when Landlady Crisp says, "Delicious meal, Farokh." She wipes her eyes, which are still watering from the fire-hot sauce.

"It was good," says Tamika.

Bape beams. "Food always tastes better when it is shared with friends," he says. "Do you not agree, Lowji?"

"Oh, yes," I say. I slip a piece of meat under the table to King, who has been drooling on my left sandal. "Food is best when it is shared."

From across the table Ma flashes her dark eyes at me. I am thinking she will scold me for feeding an animal at the table, but she says, "Do not forget about the cat, Lowji. The cat is our guest too."

At that moment Trapper springs into Tamika's lap. She licks her paws and cleans her whiskers.

"Ah," says Ma, smiling. "It appears Trapper has already eaten."

Tamika blushes.

"Then," says Bape with a clap of his hands, "we are ready for dessert."

"Wait," I say. "I want to show our friends something."

Ma sees the glass of milk in my hand. "Oh, no you don't," she says in her warning voice.

I put down the glass. "I do not want to show them *that*, Ma," I say. "I have not had enough practice to show them *that*. But maybe—"

Ma cuts off my words. "Lowji!"

I grin. Then I stand and gesture for our guests to follow me. Everyone does except King, who stays to lick drops of lentil and lamb off the tablecloth. I lead them into the kitchen, to the windowsill and my garden.

"Look," I say. I point to the pots.

Landlady Crisp and Tamika peer into them. Tiny

green plants have pushed up and out of the soil. Little leaves have opened themselves to the sun.

Tamika picks up one of the pots and gently touches a threadlike stem with her finger. The stem bends, but then springs back.

"What will they grow into?" she asks.

"Flavors from India," I say. "Green chilies. Coriander. Curry leaves. Onions."

"Really?" says Tamika. "Plants from India can grow in America?"

I nod. "They can grow and flourish."

As I say this, I can hear Jamshed.

*More silver, Lowji! More silver!*

# MY INDIAN-AMERICAN DICTIONARY

India is a country of many languages—387 of them, to be exact. And although Hindi is the official language of India, most of us do not speak it. Instead we speak our state language. For example, in the state of Bengal people speak Bengali. In Punjab they speak Punjabi. And in Bombay we spoke Gujarati. Of course, Ma and Bape and I spoke mostly English. Lots of other Indians speak mostly English too. You see, in India, English is the most commonly spoken language of all. But it is a unique sort of English because it is sprinkled with Indian words. Some of these words may be Hindi.

Some may be Gujarati. Some may even be Bengali or Punjabi. But no matter what language they come from, they work just like turmeric in white rice—adding flavor to the ordinary.

*appam*—(Hindi) a crepelike rice pancake filled with spiced meat, or potatoes and vegetables

*bakrun*—(Gujarati) a goat

*bape*—(Gujarati) dad

*bilaadi*—(Gujarati) a cat

*chai wallah*—(Hindi) a tea seller

*curry*—a very hot combination of spices, including cayenne pepper, turmeric, and fenugreek

*dhansak*—(Gujarati) a favorite Parsi dish made of lentils and lamb

*fehtna*—(Gujarati) a tall, stiff ceremonial hat

*gulab jamun*—(Hindi) golden fried cheese balls covered in honey

*halwai*—(Hindi) maker and vendor of sweet desserts and snacks

*humata, hukhta, huvarashta*—(Gujarati) good thoughts, good words, good deeds

*kusti*—(Gujarati) a ceremonial lamb's-wool belt worn by Parsis as a reminder to speak good words and think good thoughts

*kutto*—(Gujarati) a dog

*ma*—(Gujarati) mom

*maarun miithun madhurun ghar*—(Gujarati) sweet or happy home

*masala*—(Hindi) a spice mixture used on poultry, seafood, and occasionally pork

*najare padvum*—(Gujarati) we will see

*navjote*—(Gujarati) the initiation of a Parsi child into the Zoroastrian religion

*o bap re bap*—(Gujarati) thank goodness

*pista kulfi*—(Hindi) a traditional Indian ice cream flavored with pistachio nuts

*rotli*—(Gujarati) tortilla-like whole wheat bread

*rupee*—the primary unit of currency in India

*salwar kameez*—(Hindi) a long tunic (*kameez*) and loose pants (*salwar*) worn by younger Indian women

*skunkudio*—(Gujarati) "skunk" and "dio," which stands for both affection and dislike

*sudrah*—(Gujarati) a plain white cotton shirt worn by Parsis as a reminder to do good deeds

*ud*—(Gujarati) soar, fly successfully

*undardi*—(Gujarati) a mouse

*vah*—(Gujarati) bravo or good